ERRLUS

THE MAKING OF A TIME PIRATE

OTHER BOOKS BY AUTHOR

Cold Sun

Intoxication

ERRLUS

THE MAKING OF A TIME PIRATE

CATHERINE MARIE WEISS-CELLEY

ISBN: 979-8-88640-758-7 (sc)
ISBN: 979-8-88640-759-4 (hc)
ISBN: 979-8-88640-760-0 (e)

THE EWINGS
PUBLISHING

One Galleria Blvd., Suite 1900, Metairie, LA 70001
1-888-421-2397

CONTENTS

ARTWORK

Cover and all artwork listed above was created by the author to give the reader an idea of the attitudes of the characters during the intense situations described in this book. If ever this book becomes a movie, the author had hoped that someone like Jennifer Annistan could play Andrea, Brad Pitt could play Francis, Angelina Jolie: Gwendolyn, and Jayson Werth should play Errlus... if baseball could spare him.

DEDICATION

*and gratitude for the insight gathered in knowing
the following people. The lessons learned helped me
write this book. This book was written…:*

*For my children, Julia and John, and all their friends: Erica, Miranda,
Kristine M., Christine J., Christopher J., Chase, Bruce, Kelly, Bobby,
Cassie, Paul, Patrick, Anthony, Dan (please take care of yourself. You
would have been a fine son-in-law), Eric, even Matthew (the drummer
who wore his kilt proudly at 3-years old), and the rest.*

*For my ex-husband, John Celley (Falconer, Tow-Boat Captain, Fish
and Wildlife Deputy, Ham Radio Operator, Electrician, Fisherman,
Hunter, First Great Love of my Life), hope his soul finds new joy and
life and is able to aide—with God's help—the lives of those he loved.*

*For my mom: Thanks for the plus-es: The trip to Switzerland, the many
dinners, and for your gingerbread-house-making grandma status.*

*For Harry Weiss, my dad, Thanks for: the many times you fixed my car
and the "Don't stand out like an orange pea" theory.*

*For Harry, David, Eddie (so sorry about the rings), Lori, Colleen, Zoraya,
Matthew (with the tattoos), Irene and Iusley and all relatives of each.*

*For Patty (my talented, studious, hard-working sister who died from
leukemia in '76) Wish I could have known you more.*

For Mary, my aunt who was like a sister when we were young.

For Uncle Ed who was like a dad sometimes. For all my uncles and aunts, great aunts and great uncles

For my maternal grandparents (—Francis who almost became a priest, played with the Philadelphia A's [one of the Lefty's], later became a paint chemist. – His wife, Agnes, a polio survivor saved by St. Philomena Oil at 3 and saved again at 40 by having a baby [Mary, my closest aunt])

For my paternal grandparents who—after maintaining a small business in the Great Depression—survived seeing their five sons go off to war and return.

For my father-in-law, Al Celley (Wish we had more walks)

For Margaret Celley (Thanks for the Stories)

For Andy Celley (Thanks for the Hope)

For Jen (good friend and inspiration)

For Joe (her husband, my "Top Button" Critic)

For Drew and Erica (Drew: Thanks for the computer lessons way back you once-upon-a-time-"5-year-old"-genius)

For Cara and Nick – my youngest siblings (Eddie was so glad to find out he was no longer the youngest)

For my nieces and nephews: Elizabeth, David, Abigail, Zapora, and Jocelyn the painter in the family (you kindred spirit you)

For all my cousins especially Jennifer, Kimberly, Stephanie, John W. (Hope China is still your home of choice, if not, contact Brother Joe), for the late Bobby J and his son Bobby B who should be one of the main characters in a film version of this book, for Michael, Bruce, Andrea, Fiona, Bobby E.(the photographer), Joey, Debbie (who taught "Heart and Soul"), Uncle Joe's adopted children: Debbie and Donna, Donna's oldest son who died a year after she did and his young brother), Linny Burns-Sinnerard, Ruthie, Carol, Roy, Max, Tommy Burns, and all the children and relatives of these many families.

For Angela Sinnerard-Terra, my late godchild and her children: Michael Terra Jr. and E.J. and Emmit Coleman – May God guide and guard your souls and E.J. and Emmit your lives as well.

For E.J. and Emmit's father and family now, May God guide and guard your souls and lives and grant you joy and wisdom.

For Angela's first husband, Michael Terra, Sr., Michael's dad, May God guide and guard your soul and life and give you joy and wisdom. May you be blessed with love again.

For Sharon Fiorvanti Bliss and her children. (Especially Joey, Rebecca and Rachel and the little girl Harry tried to adopt and the baby born as I talked quietly to calm her frightened mother in the hospital. Your mother believed in honesty and love and was a devoted friend when she was most needed.

For Eve Kirsten Blakely.

For Rudy Valentino Vineziano (Thanks for the songs and lessons)

For Jim (my Second Great Love and his wonderfully warm family)

For the two little boys who just lost their father this August of 2011. You were the highlights of his life, you made his life worthwhile. He loved you more than himself. Your mother, for a few brief years, was the world to him, as he to her.

For the young boy who helped me learn how to play tennis when I was a teenager. I hope you are able to have choices that bring you more joy.

Thank you all for the wealth of experiences found in knowing each of you just a little. Thank you for the inspiration you have offered.

PREQUEL

THE TIME PIRATE'S FIRST TRIP

For as long as anyone could remember, after the 17-year old son of their benefactor disappeared, the daughters of their world were sent to schools that were named after their benefactor's future daughter-in-law. This was because of a prank the 17-year old's best friend played on him centuries ago. While the two boys were checking out the lab where the Time Cell was stored, the younger boy slipped in through the partly opened door. Before exiting, he hit a bunch of numbers on the control board, laughed, then ran out just as his friend tripped in through the door to see what he was doing.

Both were stunned when the opening sealed shut. The boy who was left behind, told the elders how he watched the Time Cell become transparent, then disappear. He did not know when the Time Cell would reappear.

Due to a letter written to their benefactor, sent by the man who first used the Time Cell, it became known that once the boy who tripped into the Time Cell re-emerged into history, he would meet his future wife and both of them would lead their world into existence... and prosperous, honorable adventures. For this reason, centuries of young girls fell in love with the idea of being the reason that the benefactor's son chose to stay and take on the goals that were set for him to accomplish. Most girls were given the same first name since that was all that was known of the girl who enchanted the young man so much that he gave up his family and friends for her. Schools were set up to accommodate all who wished to have a chance to be the first heiress of their world. The schools were called, "Johannah Schools".

The letter written to their benefactor also instructed him to create their series of colonies on their Earthlike moon. The letter emphasized how the boy in the Time Cell, the benefactor's eldest son, would reappear in a future time, meet the love of his life, and stay in that future time because of her; and she would become his confidant, his resting place, his best friend. She was the link that would allow for the existence of the colonies because this boy would be trained to lead his future world back to Earth in a quest to re-populate the once uninhabitable planet with volunteers from the colonies on their world. These volunteers would also be trained to deal with a scorched planet and get it to yield crops again.

Earth had been the home of all the original colonists. At a future time, when the benefactor's son would be instructed by a visitor from his past, he would send ships to the time just before the Earth caught fire like a small sun. The ships would rescue the ancestors of the colonists and bring them to their new world where air, water, animal and plant life had been secured by the Time Pirate's men for centuries before his birth. The Johannah this 17 year old would meet had to be skilled; thus, the series of schools that were set up to teach the future spouse of a future leader demanded qualified applicants. Only the brightest, most well-rounded students were mandated to attend. All who attended had to have the highest grades in the colonies. Math, Science, Psychology, Physics, Statistics, Music and Art had to be mastered. Each attendee was also taught the value of being a good wife. They were taught how to cook using vegetables grown nearby. They were taught the history of two different worlds.

They were given courses in therapy so as to learn how to temper their own goals and how to soothe the temperaments of others. Then, once they mastered their classes, in the year before they graduated, the finest students were given a week in the lab in the hope that when the son of the man who brought them to this world appeared after stumbling and then traveling in an unsecured Time Cell, he would see "the Johannah of the week", fall in love, and continue with the plans set forth by his father over 1600 years before.

Most young women looked forward to their chance to become a woman loved by a mysterious, handsome man who would have the power to command scientists, engineers, bankers, and politicians. But a few women fell in love with the education more than the myth. Their waiting week for them was not a welcome way to spend their time. It was dreaded. One such woman was in the lab that day.

She remembered how her sister came home in tears at the end of her week. She had talked about him for years before. "He's so gorgeous?" "…so noble", "so wise…" "—he loved her so much!", "I heard he moved mountains for her." "She was his reason to be." This defiant woman's broken-hearted sister, Johannah Patricia Fyre, had been in love since she had heard his story like so many girls of that time were in love with the idea and the chance to be married to someone so perfect. She, however, thought that the entire idea was annoyingly manipulative and limiting. For centuries, girls thought of him hoping their week in the lab would reap them a mythical husband. They would don their white lab coats and take their turn. She refused to go by her first name (which like the others was "Johannah"). Her name was Fiorin Fyre. She would not answer her mother till she called her Fiorin even when only her and her mother were in the room. She wanted to be a physicist. "Forget marriage!" she told her family. "Science is more important." She was anxious for her week to be over. She did not want to be just a wife to some future hero. She wanted to be known for her discoveries not just as a loved spouse.

She had dreaded the idea of meeting him: she had figured he would be spoiled and snobbish. Soon, this last day would be over, this week of mandatory waiting, and her time of being subjected to an already chosen fate, would be done. She could focus on her Physics degree without interruption. Her sister's last opportunity in the lab was met with devastation but "Fiorin Fyre", felt elated. She looked anxiously at the digital clock.

Nearly 100 people in white lab-coats were with her in the huge three-story lab. Photographers were busy trying to set-up their cameras in key locations. A young man came over to her and stated the obvious: "Your time here is almost done." To his surprise, she told him how she could not wait. "My sister was devastated when her time ended. I'll be so relieved." She looked at the door anxiously. "Why pink?" the young man asked, indicating the color of her lab coat. Fiorin stated, "I was hoping to get my mother to let me stay home by making sure all my lab coats got bleached with a red scarf. She just made me wear one. I'll be glad to just go back to studying. This waiting for a mythical husband is wasting my time."

Just then the light fluttered, and a hissing sound from the platform area started as a pinkish-golden ball appeared spinning and spraying a shower of steam and mist over the closest crowd. Everyone cheered and flashes from cameras went off like fireworks. The young man looked at "Johannah" Fiorin, and said, "I was about to ask you out…." As he looked at the emerging glowing orb, "but it looks like you're engaged." He bowed away from her.

She was horrified and wanted to escape. She walked to the nearby restroom, tried the windows, started for the door, but guards were blocking her way. Photographers started taking her picture. The golden orb stopped spinning, a door hissed open in the object, and out stepped a young boy.

He looked puzzled at all the people taking pictures and cheering. He saw a pretty girl in pink staring at him and walked toward her. She was the only one not cheering or clapping. He reached her and asked "What's all the fuss?" She looked at his handsome boyish face and suddenly realized, "his family is gone. He has no one. His mother and father, sister, brothers have been dead for centuries but to him they are still alive. He was only gone 15 minutes…."

"You don't know… do you?!" she asked incredulously.

She thought of how he would never see his family again. This stung her. How could she tell him? Her heart became overwhelmed with compassion and loss as if his family's passing brought her grief also. She took his hand and said, "Well…" She looked into his amazing eyes and was taken-back by the way he looked at her. "I have so much to tell you."

The warmth of her hand was so reassuring. She was so calm and so concerned for some reason as if some great sadness had come over her; but her smile made everything everywhere seem to have a purpose. He asked her her name. She—for the first time in her 18 years of life—said her first name proudly. "Johannah" she said. If he was her fate, predicted by folk songs, bibles, children stories, history books, she would accept whatever that fate would bring. He needed someone to show him the value of himself and the value of the work laid out for him by his father. He would be the leader that would bring them back to Earth some day. He would need a reason to believe in all he had to do. Somehow she knew she was now that reason and the innocence and joy she saw in his face when he arrived after his short journey to a new time, fascinated her. She was falling in love; and so was he. Gingerly, she led him to the door and opened it to a city he had never seen that had waited for him since the day he should have turned eighteen.

Errlus

PART I

THE MAN FROM THE PAST

CHAPTER 1

3031 YEARS AND BACK

Bernard in 2052 – Bernard in the year 5092

They carried the dying man into the future.

The spinning of the time capsule seemed too intense for Jonas. He checked the instruments while careful not to move from where he had secured himself for the 3031-year ride.

Andrea noticed her partner's concern. The sedative they initialized upon securing their "patient" was wearing off. She looked at Bernard. He looked in pain but stable.

"So much depends on him." She said.

Jonas Acknowledged. "Yes. I just hope—" he paused a moment worrying about the possibilities. "Ah, this trip, the children. Is he the answer?" He shook his head and shut his eyes.

"His music survived over 3000 years. They listen to it, dance, try to imitate it. He has inspired so many even after his death—he *must* have an impact on them." She looked over at the hunchbacked, white-haired man sleeping in the timecell chair between them. Tumors covered his face and scalp. His fingers were bent, his clothes were singed, the timecell smelt of sweat and smoke. Could he make her son want to live again? she wondered.

"So many have died. And the ones that want to live seem to worship that pirate that risks existence itself with his network of thieves. This world—that man must have no sense of the danger he's causing."

"I take it you mean Errlus."

"Yes, Errlus. How far back has he reached? The first recorded documents salvaged from the ancient colonies before we even knew about time travel mention his name. And now he's stealing cargo from our ships. It's a wonder we all haven't disappeared out of existence totally."

"Why do you suppose he's such a hero to them?"

"Children—teenagers—they are being led. At least it's a suspicion I have. He's like a pied piper to crime. Perhaps Bernard here can teach them to enjoy life without them attempting to join Errlus's crew of—" Jonas's head was pounding. "pirates, mobsters, low-life peddlars of... history."

Andrea looked at her tired, angry friend. "Rest. Bernard's the key. His music makes a person want to live. He'll be the new hero of our time. Once our doctors cure him, I'll bet he'll even be handsome."

"Hope we got to him in time."

"Yes, if he dies again, we'll have to reposition the timecell and that fire—There's not many more places to land the cell in that inferno.:

"We got to him in time." Jonas said with a willful certainty. As if his will could make it happen.

"He has to live—for the children." Added Andrea.

Jonas looked at the pain-strewn features of his kidnapped patient. Was he the savior that would keep his daughter from trying to kill herself? He undid one of his straps to his chair so as to pinch his eyebrows in an attempt to alleviate the pressure behind his eyes. "Yes," he said as he squinted his eyes shut trying not to imagine his 28-year old daughter stepping into the NR3. "...for the children."

The years went by quickly.

CHAPTER 2

BERNARD HOPKINS

The people waited anxiously. Some wanted to see the time cell appear. Some wanted to get a glimpse of the leader of their continent. Some wanted to see the musician she rescued from the past. Some wanted to see the golden-haired, handsome, richest man in their hemisphere emerge from his trip to the year 2059. Pink clouds formed above the pedastal. There was a crack of lightening and a spinning roar of sound that started just as a gold sun-like object appeared above them on the inverted cone of liquid that splattered the protective glass bowl beneath it in a spray of mist that made a small rainbow of color.

The egg-shaped vessel spun in the pool for almost 20 minutes. A flat, ring-shaped platform was raised to encompass the perimeter of its base. A searing sound hissed as an opening melted away into the space of an entrance. Out stepped Jonas and Andrea as a team of doctors rushed in. Jonas stood at the pedastal before the crowd as they waved and applauded. Jonas went to the microphone provided.

"Bernard Hopkins is with us." He looked over at the doctors as they gave him the signal. ...and he's very much alive."

The crowd cheered. Most of them had children who signed up for the NR3, the third death chamber of its kind, a room where the living became nothing. A person could go inside, press a button, and disappear from existence in a flash of electricity. Once they were of age, it was legal. The only way to stop them was to make them want to live. That was getting to be more and more difficult. Suicide was an epidemic of the time. Parents were desperate for a way to help their children enjoy life. For centuries the candidates for the chamber increased in number. Then, 30 years ago a safe was opened which held ancient marble recording disks containing music, plays and art from the 21st century. Bernard Hopkins' music became the most popular of the collection. Young men and women began to take their names off the list. Each person who cancelled their appointment with death was noted to have secured a large collection of Bernard's work.

It had been the Council's goal to rescue the well-known playwright and musician, Bernard Hopkins, from a fiery death that claimed his life in the year 2059. It was a risky mission. No one had ever been known to travel that far back before. The distance in years was deemed to allow a change in history to occur. Since Bernard was recorded to have died at that time in a house fire, there was not much chance of history being changed by his disappearance. It would be an experiment in time travel as well as the beginning of a program to help young people find a new passion for life.

Jonas Doucet was selected for this mission due to his knowledge of time travel and his adherence to the rules. He was the CEO of the Time Cell Corporation. His daughter was still on the NR3 list even after Bernard's music had become popular.

Andrea Anderson volunteered so as to find a way to help her son, Popla, deal with his suicidal turn. He had been devastated at the loss of his first love, a woman who—to Andrea and to many of her associates—appeared to be the most beautiful woman they had ever seen. She was stunning. Olivia had perfect poise and grace and her voice was mesmerizingly like a fine musical instrument that once heard, made a listener anxious to hear more. She was attracted to Popla, Andrea's son, for some reason that Andrea could not imagine.

They were a beautiful couple. They were engaged until one day Olivia saw a newspaper article with Errlus's picture on the front page. He became all she would talk about. She learned about his syndicate, his quoted phrases, his elaborate thefts that would make any business that was victimized by Errlus' syndicate, wealthier in less than a year. She was so infatuated that when she learned she was pregnant with Popla's child, she underwent the procedure that removed the fetus from her body for storage in a cryogenic lab. She told Popla that she was not ready to be a mother yet. She became less accessible. Then, she wrote a note to Popla explaining how she had to leave to follow her dreams. She "had loved him for so long" she wrote "but that had changed"; and she needed to follow her heart.

Popla stopped eating. He slept in the day. Walked the streets at night, was found sleeping on doorsteps, on sidewalk benches. He grew paler and distant. He talked as if his mind was somewhere else. Andrea would look in his eyes as he sat by a window staring and it seemed he was looking at something no one else could see. Then he signed up for the NR3 and she knew she might lose her son forever. Bernard's music seemed to make him more responsive. He even tried to learn the flute to play the music. Then he would hear something about Errlus and he would grow despondent again. Errlus had taken Olivia's love away from him and there was no way he could compare to a man with that much power.

Popla had to be force fed intravenously on two occasions. Andrea was desperate. When she heard about the "The Man From the Past" project and the scarcity of adequate travelers for the mission, she volunteered. She had been training five people to take over her job for more than a decade in the hope to retire soon. Her responsibilities could be handled without her for a few months if need be. This project would give her a chance to save someone she loved more than herself. Before volunteering, she surmised that being a governor of one of the largest continents in the world should be enough credentials for the Council to approve her application and she already knew the other volunteer for the mission.

Jonas was a close friend of her husband's; she knew him well and had a great respect for his work ethic and discipline. His only flaw appeared to be that he was too disciplined. She knew of how grief-stricken Gwendolyn had been after the accident that claimed the lives of her husband and son. She knew Jonas had the ability to send someone back in time to stop Gwendolyn's son and husband from taking that fatal drive on that cold wintry day. Just by stopping them from driving the route they had chosen would have saved their lives; but Jonas believed this would cause a detrimental, possibly apocalyptal effect on all life and history, so he refused to save his son-in-law and grandson even after his daughter signed up for the NR3.

Andrea was surprised Jonas even allowed this project to take place. Perhaps she could persuade him to change his mind about using time travel to change *recent* events. She mentioned it to him a number of times as they were traveling to rescue Bernard but Jonas was adamant. No one could go back in time to change history within a thousand years of the starting date of a mission, not even himself. She could tell by his face how he wished he could go back to save his grandson but he believed it would cancel the existence of all things. Errlus, he knew, had done this and still society continued on after all his thefts of ships and freight cars, abductions of people, bank account manipulations, plane heists—but Jonas believed the ramifications caused by Errlus did not yet occur and as the head of the Time Cell Corporation, he could not promote the rescue of his family without thousands of other grieving families making desperate demands for changing time. He could not take the chance of saving two by risking the loss of everyone and everything.

Andrea thought about this and how ridiculous it seemed as she walked to the mike to comment on Bernard's condition but once she reached the podium, she sank to her knees as the world seemed to spin out from under her and she fell to unconsciousness.

CHAPTER 3

EIGHT SUNS

There was fire everywhere. The heat seemed to suck out the air from his lungs. Two large dark objects pulled him, dragged him into a cool egg-shaped glowing object. Were they feeding him to this creature? He wondered, but he didn't care, it felt cooler. Then the mouth shut with a searing noise and the two feeders were belting him in as the room spun. His chest felt compressed. He vomited; he couldn't breathe. Someone reached over to tilt his head. He could breathe again, but his chest was tight; then this woman was breathing into his mouth and counting, breathing into him and counting. The pain went away and he fell asleep. He was lying on clouds it seemed. The dawn was coming as the sky glowed bright with light. There were eight suns. A voice as deep as any baritone boomed like thunder. "Bernard," it called to him. "Can you hear me Bernard."

"Yes—, yes." He said as he tried to turn his head. Above him loomed the giant bearded face of a curly-haired man amidst the eight suns or were they stars. "Yes. I hear you."

The voice boomed, "You cannot imagine how good it is to see you doing so well Bernard. As soon as you can, I have a number of people that want to meet you."

The thunderous voice rang in his mind as he looked straight ahead and noticed the stars turning into lights. The cloud he was on was actually the softest bed he had ever felt and the voice and golden-haired man looming above him still glowed magnificently.

"Do you have any questions, Bernard."

"Yes." He said.

"Go ahead. Ask me anything."

Bernard looked at the glowing hair before the eight lights and carefully, respectfully asked, "Are you…" he paused afraid to ask for a moment, "Are you… –God?"

The godly being smiled. "No" he laughed. "But I can understand how you might think that, after what you have been through. No, I am a person just like you who believes—perhaps unlike you—that you have the gift of life itself to share."

The sound of a cart echoed in the room as a tray of food was wheeled in.

"We have much to talk about Bernard, but for now, get stronger; and enjoy your dinner. You have been here three days now. Drink first, then eat slow, rest and soon we'll talk again."

Jonas left the room feeling jubilant and somehow grateful. His mission, so far, did not have any negative ramifications. The world seemed brighter.

He walked down to the next corridor and knocked on the hospital room door. The nurse there greeted him and stated that he should not stay long but Andrea insisted upon seeing him.

"Sleep becomes you. You gave us all a scare." Jonas said as he entered his fellow time-traveler's hospital room.

"They tell me it's an iron deficiency. I'm just glad it's not an end of the world as we know it. How are you?"

"Very well, thank you. I just wanted to be the first to tell you that Bernard Hopkins is well; and very much confused." He laughed as he looked at his pale, bed-ridden partner and added, "He thinks I'm God".

Andrea laughed. "Well, cure my anemia then she said." Jonas agreed as her cheeks seemed to flush.

"I'll tell Dominick he can see you in the morning. Can you believe it: I've known you for thousands of years more than your husband has known you? We're just about related." He smiled at her as he insisted, "Rest now and don't ever scare me like that again."

Andrea asked, "How's Popla?"

"He's fine. He's with Dominick. They had dinner together. He seems more himself. This Bernard trip... it may just work.

CHAPTER 4

15 STORIES UP

Mythology:
A Queen Contemplates Death Over Subjugation

The night air was clear and cool. She looked up at the moon and shut her eyes while holding out her arms shoulder high to her sides. Just a little further, just one more step and she would be gone. She looked straight ahead at the empty world before her. Strawberry blonde waves of hair framed her face. Emerald green eyes glared out at the sunset. She stood—like a doomed queen in the children's story she had read as a child—balancing herself on the edge of the 15-story building contemplating the alternative to life as if it were the better choice.

Her husband and son had died in a fire that melted half a city block into molten beams, pulverized concrete, burnt plastic. Would she see them again she wondered? Just one step further, she thought. She lifted her foot; then she saw a sllight movement below her about two buildings away. A squat, little man walked into a wall and apologized to it, then broke out laughing so hysterically that he had to balance himself with his hand on the wall. Then he leaned closer to the wall as he bent his elbow to get a better look. As he extended his arm again, he put his head down, and began sobbing... or was it laughing. She noticed his shoulders heave up and down as the wavy-haired man stared at his feet. She listened intently as the wind died. He was laughing, looking at the wall, then laughing. Then he righted himself, brushed himself off, looked around while still chuckling to himself but seeming somewhat embarrassed, then, he walked on toward the lecture hall. He must be the lecturer her father had told her to see that night. What could make a person laugh so much she wondered.

She stepped back from the ledge, started toward the stairs, figured she would save the world a little mess for awhile and see about this strange little man who laughed at nothing. She envied him this stilted pleasure that was now so evasive to her sentiments. She would attend the lecture out of curiosity even though she hated the idea that it was like obeying her cold-hearted father. Perhaps she could begin to feel again somehow at this meeting. She missed being able to laugh. For the first time in months she grew hopeful.

The lecture hall was packed. The seats circled the stage area where a piano had been placed to be lit by two crossing beams of amber light. Gwendolyn was surprised at how many people were in the audience. She had heard that only those scheduled for the NR3 were to attend that night. Somehow she felt vindicated in her signing up for the Nothingness Room as she saw how many other kindred spirits surrounded her. People were shuffling into seats. Some people were wondering out loud why they had come.

A tall man with a thin mustache introduced Bernard after a short bio.

Gwendolyn was surprised to learn that Bernard had actually been hunchbacked at one time. She had heard some of his music. The lights got dim and a lone light centered on a platform door. Bernard walked out. His head was down. He carried his music case the 46 steps to the piano. He put the case down, went to the mike, looked out at the audience, shook his head, went back to the piano, took out music, put it away, then rested his hands upon the keys for almost a solid minute without sound, then, he shut his eyes and began to play.

He could make a piano sound like a rainstorm. His hands went up and down the keys quicker than most people could wave. He pounded out notes like hammers hitting metal drums. He seemed to get the notes to say, "Live, Live, Live" over and over again. One two-minute segment sounded like love first found, another sounded like dishonor and humiliation, another sounded like triumph over tyranny, then there was fear, then loss, then discord and harmony taking turns. Gwendolyn saw her life in his music. Tears filled her eyes as she remembered when she first found out that her husband had fallen for another woman. Then in a loud moment of notes pounded out in anger mixed with a steady trickle of solid sounding high notes trickled out like a plea, Bernard stopped playing. The room was icily silent. Then one by one people stood up and started clapping. Many of them were crying. Bernard went to the mike.

He bowed his head to acknowledge them then said, "I had prepared a speech, but when I saw all of you... beautiful people, and knew that each of you had given up on living, all I could do was play out the anguish at the loss of what your lives could be."

He surveyed the crowd again. Each person was beautiful. They looked like models in this new age of technological wonders, gene therapy and plastic surgery that created perfect symmetry and proportion in anyone who opted for the operations or treatments. They all looked perfect.

"I see perfection in you. Each of you would be movie star material in my time. The question that slaps me in the face as I look at each one of your faces is, 'Why?' 'Why?' 'Why do you want to throw it all away.' Don't you see what you have here.? You have perfection all around you. Reach for it, embrace it.

"My sister...." He put his head down. "She committed suicide," he paused "a long time ago. You see her fiancee broke off their engagement... after meeting me. Back then, oh, well, up to about six months ago for me, I was a cripple..." The audience gasped. Some of them did not know what that was. Some did and explained.

"Yes, I was a hunch-backed cripple." He bent over and put a large, bunched-up handkerchief into the back left side of his shirt to create a lump; then, he hobbled across the stage. "I could hardly walk. I used a cane most of the time. And that wasn't the worst of it. I had lumps, the size of a baby's fist, all over my body. Some of them were red, some purplish brown, with hair growing out of them and where there weren't lumps, there were folds of skin, wrinkles like an elephant's knees in the most cumbersome places. I had to have surgery to lift the folds from my eyes. This was difficult but still I felt this drive to create something beautiful, to tell stories of things or of people I fell in love with, but when my sister left me that note saying how her Freddy left her because he was afraid she might have the gene that I had... well. First I wanted to knock that fellow flat; but I had a funeral to attend to, a memory to honor, a loved one to pray for. I am sure most of you have just as much love in your lives as I did through my sister, through my co-workers, through my friends. Don't you know how devastated they would feel? How alone? Achingly alone your friends or family would be without you. It's like part of the world is gone. A house where you know friends are becomes a shell, a tease of lost solace. When someone you love chooses to die rather than be with you or because of you, or both, you start after a while to have moments of hate for that person, brief moments, that you regret having later when the sadness sets in again or a good, happy memory trickles into your consciousness. Surely you all must have had at least one time when you were happy." He looked at the frozen crowd to whom he was pleading.

One tall man waved his hand like a wind-blown leaf. Bernard pointed to him and he stood up. In an aristocratic voice that bordered on monotone out of what seemed to be boredom, the man said, "They closed the NR3. When will it be opened again."

Bernard was shocked that the news of the closing had spread already. He looked at the tall man and said, "Not until the prerequisite is completed. Each of you will receive a copy of the music I just played. In order to qualify for the… chamber—you must create a story-line, an artwork, a piece of music or dance that comes close to what this music depicts. Once that is done, the person who creates this work will have permission to enter, the NR3. This way, the people you know and who perhaps love you will have something positive from your life and this way—I hope—you will learn to change your minds."

The tall man turned to leave without a word. He left in disgust it seemed.

"Any other questions," Bernard asked while not really expecting any from this lifeless crowd. A woman stood up a few rows from where he stood. She was exquisite. "Yes, Mr. Hopkins, can you tell me more about the year you wrote this music." There were tears in her eyes he noticed. They glistened like jewels and fell from her chin. He was surprised to see such pain in the face of such a beauty who lived in this age that he had thought was perfect socially and technologically.

"Yes, of course, Miss—"

"Mrs" She corrected. Mrs. Montgomery."

Jonas's daughter he thought. He answered her questions while trying not to seem as enchanted as he had suddenly become. "The year was actually just three years after my sister's death and five years before my own near death occurrence. That would be 2054. The crowd gasped. Bernard added with a laugh. "Yes, I am a very, very old man: perhaps the oldest alive, except for Errlus. I'm told he may be older."

"Thank you, sir." Said Mrs. Montgomery… as she wrote the year on her palm.

"You are most welcome. Any other questions?" No one raised a hand. Some had started to walk out. "Please pick up your copy of the music played tonight in the baskets at the back. Another copy will be mailed to your place of residence. If you care to have a video of tonight's performance, that will be available on line at the Time Cell Corporation's website. My office is in the Shevly building down the street from the Time Cell Building. Please drop in if you need help with your presentations. My goal is to help you with your goal to achieve completion of the prerequisite. I believe it will change your mind about life but I am honor-bound to respect your achievements if your work models the music fairly well. Any other questions….?"

Still, no one raised a hand. The seats were being bumped and jostled. Bernard said as they were leaving, "Well if you have no other questions yet, I'll just play the piano while you leave… for a while." Some sat down to listen while letting the others clear the walkways. Gwendolyn was one of the ones who remained. The music had made her remember the most poignant times in her life: the good and the bad. It was good to feel again although her heart felt heavy and her eyes would not stop tearing. She listened to Bernard play till all the attendees had left. They turned out the lights on her. Bernard stopped playing. He just looked at the keyboard; then, he picked up his music sheets and started for the exit. She watched him leave. Then the stage lights went out. After a while she rose and headed home.

Tomorrow, she would go to her father's Time Cell Corporation and look up the year 2054 to learn more about the time that could have inspired someone to write music like what she had heard Bernard play. She was sure there was not much information left from that time, but whatever could be found would be at the archives.

The streets outside did not seem as dismal as they had been when she had entered the lecture hall. They appeared almost colorful. She walked by the building that she almost jumped from and felt so relieved that she had not taken that last step. Bernard's funny apologetic, clutzy way had saved her, she thought. Perhaps some day she would tell him how. Now all she wanted was sleep and another day to study an ancient time.

CHAPTER 5

··
THE FIREPLACE
··

P opla had not gone to the lecture. Andrea had told him to go and invited him to a late dinner of his favorite foods. She had told him that she had something important to tell him and his father. She had figured a nice dinner and some drinks might soften the news about her new assignment.

Popla was early.

Andrea was surprised that the lecture had left out so soon but she was glad that her son had thought enough to come to the dinner without a reminder from her.

He came into their suite as if the fire in their fireplace drew him there. He was cold. Somehow he had tripped into a fountain in front of the hotel where his mother and father were staying. He had been staring at the moon and tried to walk to it up the steps before the multi-colored fountain and then suddenly, he fell. He had stood there a while in water up to his knees while looking at the moon as droplets streamed down his face. Then he climbed out of the fountain and entered the hotel lobby, went to the elevator and pushed the buttons to the penthouse suite while curious onlookers just stared at the puddle forming at his feet. A child asked if it was raining outside. Popla barely heard the other people in the elevator.

He saw the child's face and almost cried. He forced a smile and shook his head saying "No."

Once inside his parent's apartment he felt cold. He went to the fireplace which had a low flame to take off the evening chill. Andrea walked in with a glass of wine for her son.

"Ah Popla, I have a chilled wine for you." She went to his side as he leaned on the mantel staring at the fire. "Here's your drink."

Popla did not reach out or acknowledge the glass, he just stared into the fire. "Do you think wood feels pain as it burns?" He asked.

Andrea then realized her son was soaking wet even though there wasn't a cloud in the sky. She gulped her drink down and said. "No... that thought never crossed my mind. Sounds poetic but I'm sure many people would have a hard time starting fires if they believed *that* could happen."

Popla stared at the fire as the smoke billowed up the chimney. He added, "Some people think that smoke is actually the souls of burnt wood being carried to the sky—" Popla's right hand rested on the mantel as his left hand reached out to the flames as if to touch it. His forehead was resting on his right arm as he stared at the burning embers, smoldering beneath him. "So many souls..." he said.

Andrea rolled her eyes at her son's sense of drama and drank his wine as well. "Ah, Popla, you are drenched, let me get you a blanket." She put their glasses on the mantel. Then took his hand and led him to a rocker near the fire and sat him down like a dazed child. His hands were ice cold but his forehead was burning with fever.

"They all burned you know. Can a fetus feel fire? He asked." He seemed delirious. Andrea left the room to get him a blanket. When she returned Dominick was kneeling over her son as he lay unconscious by the chair. He was yelling, "How many Popla? How many did you take?" He was shaking his unconscious son between yelling that question, "How many?" Andrea grabbed her phone and called an ambulance. Dominick was holding a pill bottle that seemed empty. He tried to gently lift his son's face toward him asking, "How many did you take? Tell me, listen, stay awake?

Andrea went to Popla and moved the chair away while making a pillow of the blanket she brought out for him.

Did he even go to the lecture? She wondered. Dominick kept moving him, stroking his brow, pinching his ear, yelling his name, then he turned to Andrea and said. "That cryogenic lab that held that fetus of Olivia's burned to the ground two weeks ago. I thought Popla knew but he must have just found out tonight. I think he took a whole vile of these pills. Keep talking to him in different tones and help me get these wet clothes off of him."

Andrea assisted her harried husband wondering all the while if their son was dying. Tomorrow she had been scheduled to leave to check on a hijacked ship that vanished from the ocean. It disappeared on a clear day leaving nothing but pink clouds, a sign of a time vessel. Her biggest worry that night had been how could she tell her family that she had to leave. Now her only concern was their lives. Her husband had a bad heart and he was frantic. She used her most calming tone.

"He will be fine. He is stronger than we think. Just talk to him Dominick. Hold his hand. Tell him that his child will "be" again. Tell him that Olivia will be back soon. Tell him he is loved as much as he loved that unborn baby of his and he has to be here for us. He'll hear us. Just keep telling him so he hears something. It will keep him with us longer; I am sure. Be positive when you speak, there is power in it. Will him to stay with us and believe. It will help. Be calm. He will be fine."

The ambulance came quickly. They rushed him onto a stretcher. Dominick and Andrea went with them to the hospital. She would postpone the trip for a day or two, then she would have to ask friends to watch over her husband and visit her son. She would have to go to inspect the area where the vessel disappeared. The Council had mandated the trip and it was treason to refuse, plus she knew it was necessary to learn if Errlus could be proved finally to have used time travel on a vessel as large as an ocean liner. That was impossible according to their studies but perhaps Errlus had somehow created a technological system to move large vessels into some type of a worm hole. If so, could that worm hole threaten other ships and people. Someone else should go to investigate. She would request it, but if not, she would have to leave her suicidal son and her wonderfully sensitive husband alone with only the intermittant care of strangers. Two days was all she could count on but she would try for more.

CHAPTER 6

GOLDEN MINES

"Errlus!" "Errlus!" "Errlus!"

The crowd yelled his name like a mantra. He stepped onto the platform and raised his arms. The crowd quieted down.

"Good news." He said. "The mines are secured and as expected, there is much gold!"

The crowd roared. This meant the developments would get their much needed supplies soon. More time cells could be built to reach the older colonies. History could be continued. Celebrations began almost immediately. Confetti was thrown. Champagne was poured. Errlus left the group while his guards secured his path. He was exhausted.

The physical activity of travel on the rocky moon made communication difficult unless a person could run and climb extremely well. Errlus was as fit as any trained soldier but the last climb he attempted knocked the wind out of him. The stress he felt at the top of the cliff at the edge of the camp made his world a momentary nightmare. He saw his wife kiss another man. Or was it that she had been kissed. She immediately slapped the fellow's face but her coy attitude and calm voice made him wonder if it was part of a game to keep the fellow's interest. He watched her tell the man to leave and the sergeant grabbed her hand and kissed her wrist like he had done it before. *Then* he left.

Johannah did not even balk. She stepped back but just a small step and then she looked confused. Was he losing his wife... or did he already lose her? They had been arguing more. How could he continue traveling from colony to colony without her beside him?

The air around him became stale and scarce. He let himself slip down the side of the cliff and sat motionless till the other moon glowed down on the campsite. He would go home to separate himself from Johannah for a while. He could not force her to be with him. She would have to decide. If he stayed while she was *deciding* someone might just get hurt. He had to leave. He left the encampment that night and headed back to his ocean hideout.

His bed was a welcome sight. He stripped off his dusty clothes and climbed into the shower stall. He did not see the figure standing in the shadows.

He let the water massage his pounding forehead and closed his eyes to feel the power of the pulsing water against his pounding brow. He did not see the hand reaching for the curtain. His mind was on his wife's suspected infidelity. He stepped back to reach for the shampoo just as someone lunged slightly forth in back of him. A hand reached around his side to press his chest against the naked form of a full-breasted woman. Johannah never surprised him like this. He turned to face his seductress with a feint hope it was her but no. The woman pushed her body against his as she kissed his shoulder and tried to press herself to him while pushing on the vertebrae of his back with the palm of her hand. He ripped the shower curtain as he tore away from her then grabbed her elbow and pulled her toward the bed. Then he threw a robe around the dripping wet form of the silly young woman and did his best not to slap her or anything else as he pulled her toward the door.

"You empty-headed selfish, impudent home wrecking—" He looked at her face for the first time. "—beauty". She was the most beautiful woman he had ever seen: golden blonde hair, pale pink lips, cornflower blue eyes, flushed cheeks, smoothe creamy complexion and perfectly voluptuous form. He hesitated; then, pulled her to the door and practically threw her into the hallway while throwing the robe out as well. "Get away from me you lovesick puppy." He growled.

Olivia stood in the hallway dripping wet and totally naked. She picked up the robe and barely covered herself as she passed by the guards. She had seen him without anything between her and him and he was all that she had expected. He might not be ready for her yet but he would change his mind. She had tracked his whereabouts ever since the ship she was on was hijacked. She even took a ride on that particular ship with the hope that it would be hijacked by Errlus's crew so that she would eventually see him. Now all she would have to do is give him some time. His wife was not around yet. She would have a few more weeks before his next mission. Then, she would try again.

CHAPTER 7

WRISTS AND GLASS

The hospital looked amazingly white. He found himself wanting to shade his eyes. He took out his sunglasses and walked through the corridors toward Popla's room. He did not notice young nurses trying to watch him from the corners of their eyes.

Bernard had become a celebrity. The surgeries he had undergone to correct his elephantism had revealed him to be attractive. He was not used to attention for such a reason so he did not acknowledge it. He figured the stares, the smiles, the generous natures exhibited were how all people were treated.

Popla's room was darker than the hallway. Bernard could barely see. He put his glasses in the case.

Andrea's son was asleep it seemed as Bernard walked in. His arm hung off the edge of the bed. A tube of clear solution was being dripped into him as he slept. Bernard remembered his own stay at the hospital. He rubbed his wrists as if he could feel the liquid pulsing through the tube. He tripped on a cup that had been knocked onto the floor and Popla woke up. Popla saw the bag of liquid hanging from the pole and looked at the clear plastic cylinder linked to his wrist. He pulled it out and threw it away from him. Blood started dripping from his arm.

"They all died you know."

Bernard went to the bed beside Popla and rang for a nurse. "No, I didn't know." He said. "Who died?"

"The babies." Popla said. "The unborn babies in the lab. No one even told me. Over 1000 babies burned. And one of them was mine."

Bernard noticed the blood dripping from Popla's arm had slowed to a trickle but he still was alarmed and went to the door to motion for a nurse to come quicker. Just as he got to the door, a nurse came in and non-chalantly went over to Popla with tape and gauze. Bernard figured that Popla must have pulled out the I.V. before.

Popla looked at Bernard inquisitively. "How can a cryogenic lab burn?" he asked. Bernard couldn't answer.

Popla added. "It's ice. Frozen children... waiting for a life that never came. How could it have burned?"

The nurse tied Popla's arms to the side of the bed saying she would be back soon.

"They tie me like a prisoner. All I want is freedom. Pills. Not the answer. Next time—"

Popla looked out the window longingly and raised his arms up while pulling on the restraints. His left restraint came undone and he pulled himself out of the bed to look at a blue vase of pink flowers. He stared at the royal blue glass as if it were the most important thing in the world. As if it were a precious dinosaur egg or life itself. Then he raised it up and crashed it on the ledge of the window. He clung to the biggest piece he could find and said over and over again, "Wrists and glass, man from the past." As he fingered the blue glass between his cut fingers and looked for a certain area in his right wrist.

"No. Popla! Nurse—" Bernard screamed as he ran to Popla's hand and pulled the hand with the blue glass away from the wrist it was aiming for. "No Popla. Don't you know what it would do to your father, to your mother. You're their only child, like that frozen baby was yours."

Popla heard this and arched his back as he pulled at the other restraint and cried in anguish. A nurse ran into the room as Popla tried to fight off Bernard. Another nurse entered with a chemical smelling wad of cotton. She tried to put it on Popla's face as Popla elbowed her in the teeth. Bernard managed to get him to drop the blue glass then he held Popla's elbows down on the bed as orderlies started entering the room with a jacket and a doctor came in with a sedative.

Popla was kicking and screaming.

"Do you think my mother cares? She's on another of her "Save the World" missions. Do you think she cares? She didn't even tell me about the lab. There's other ways to leave this world. They can't keep me here forever. There's nothing left. Nothing. Wrists and glass, man from the past." Bernard winced with pain as he heard Popla scream this.

"You don't know what your saying Popla."

"Don't I?" Popla asked but changed his tone as he noticed Bernard was overcome by something. Bernard's eyes were filled with tears.

"What don't I know Bernard? Everything's gone. Wrists and Glass. It's the only way." A needle went into his arm and his world got slower.

"Wrists and glass! Knives! I'll find a way! There's nothing!" Bernard headed for the door trying to get away from a memory. Popla saw that his visitor was upset and had to know why. He yelled to him: "Bernard—?!" in such a way that Bernard stopped to listen.

"Yes Popla." He said without turning around. Tears were dripping from his face: he did not want Popla to see how upset he was for fear that it would just bring more taunts from Popla in his semi-drugged state.

"What does that mean to you Bernard?" He saw how the words stung him so he directed the words to him again. "Wrists and glass…. Wrists and glass—who was it. Who left you, Bernard. Who?! Can a man as cold as you feel?"

Bernard had to leave the room.

"Rest, Popla. Love is not something you alone feel. Rest so you can undestand again. I have to go." He rushed out and just started walking. He must have walked down two corridors before he realized where the elevator was. He saw the stairs and took them, bounding down the steps two at a time, then bending over on the landings to catch his breath. The image of his sister in her hotel room next to the note she left. The grey skin. The void of another person gone. His stomach seemed to heave. His throat was so dry he thought he would gag. The air seemed non-existent. Finally he got to the exit door. He rushed outside and just walked as fast as he could. He took huge steps toward the entrance looking for a taxi but he couldn't flag one yet. He walked past the entrance just as a taxi stopped and a beautiful woman stepped out in a sultry, cocktail dress. The air seemed to disappear again as he stared at her without thinking.

"Ah Bernard" the woman said. "I was just going to see Popla." She said as she paid the cab driver.

It was Gwendolyn. Jonas's daughter. Somehow she looked so... different thought Bernard. Her words seemed to pull him back from the memory of his sister. His words came out of his mouth in measured syllables holding back anger and repulsion.

"Popla... does not need company... right now. He— He had to be sedated."

Gwendolyn noticed the distain Bernard seemed to have at the mention of Popla.

"Ah, he's gotten worse, then, I guess."

"At this point, I don't know if he ever was better." Bernard tried to smile.

"He does have a way of making a person... uneasy, sometimes."

"That's an understatement." Bernard's hand was stinging. He shook it to shake off the sensation. It was bleeding slightly.

"Bernard! What happened?!"

"Popla broke a vase and tried to slash his wrists." Bernard closed his eyes trying not to remember his sister.

"Ah Bernard, let's go back in and try to bandage this."

"No. No, I am fine; it's nothing."

Gwendolyn grabbed his hand with both of hers. "Please Bernard. I know hospitals are sometimes oppressive. I know a place where you can get a great dressing and a good cup of tea PLUS, there's a piano. Come on, let's get a cab."

Her hands were warm and soft as silk. And her perfume drew him closer. Instinctively, he tried to breathe more of it in. She was enchanting.

She hailed a cab. Bernard thought to himself how calming she was. She was like a gift. She chatted lightly all the way to her apartment while holding a hankerchief on his hand. Whoever the fellow she was intending to meet that night was…, he was a very lucky man.

"I hope you're not calling off your date for what seems is a paper cut?"

"My date—Oh no. I was just coming from… dinner… with a friend." She had actually been hoping to meet Bernard and ask him to join her for a drink but this was better.

"Well. Thank you for taking me under your wing. Sometimes," he thought of his sister for a moment, "it is good not to be alone."

"Yes Bernard. And that Popla. You must tell me more of what happened but first let's get you some tea." The cab stopped at her apartment and she helped Bernard out of the cab. The sky was a midnight blue. The moon was huge. Bernard's hand throbbed almost as much as his head but he longed to see this piano she spoke of and wondered how enchanting Gwendolyn's apartment would be. The tea would be a soothing treat. His throat was dry.

She brought biscuits and water to the table after she bandaged his hand. Bernard sat at the piano as she got the tea. They talked about Andrea and her father, about his sister and his music. He played tunes that he created as jingles. Then he just played. Gwendolyn found the music so soothing. She put her head down to listen and started to dream. Bernard stopped playing and just looked at her. Strawberry blonde hair, rose-petal-pink lips and her whole apartment had a scent he wished he could take with him. He wished he could kiss her hand in thanks. Instead, he left a small note, sipped some tea and called a cab. She did not hear him when he left.

PART II

ERRLUS

CHAPTER 8

A SHIP'S LURE

The sound of waves hitting the ship seemed to dull her senses. The rhythm of the water lured her into thinking about the dire situation she left behind. The constant pattern had the gentle side to side rocking of a cradle or of heartbeats to Andrea: so many heartbeats away from her family. Poor Popla, thought Andrea.

The captain of the ship and Andrea were talking about their families while gazing toward the direction of the last known distress signal. A vessel had recently disappeared from the ocean without much more than an obscure radio message. Andrea was feeling trapped by her job and angry at herself for leaving. For this reason, she spoke freely with the navy man beside her: she was anxious for some hint of understanding and approval from a person with similar commitments.

"To Popla, I must seem like an irresponsible mother." She said this with a speculative laugh as if it was ironic that a son could accuse his mother of being irresponsible.

"Children often think of their parents as inadequate in some way. My May Lou, she's always telling me I'm never there for her, that I don't care. She doesn't realize that this job is what puts her through college. Sometimes, though, she writes to me and says, 'Dear best dad in all the oceans,' I *think* that's meant as a compliment."

"My son, he hasn't said anything like that since... since he was 16-years old. Independence became too important to him. He didn't want to fraternize with what he began to see as a curious warden. This last episode though..." Andrea shook her head as she almost rested it on the railing.

"Hey, you okay?" The captain wondered if sea-sickness had set in.

"Yes, it's just... he attempted suicide before I left... the old fashioned kind."

The captain's eyes glared at Andrea. He was looking for a sign of humor on a subject that should not be amusing. Then he looked around for a member of the crew, and excused himself as he walked to a nearby sailor. He whispered, "Get Errlus on the radio, immediately." He went back to Andrea.

"Get Errlus on the Phone!"

"Do you think you could have done anything for him by being there?" he asked.

"I don't know. Sometimes I think my presence makes him worse. I'm not sure, but I can't seem to think of much else I could have done. I asked a very intuitive friend of mine to look over him— Bernard Hopkins, the musician and playwright Jonas and I brought from the Past. He has a way with most of the suicide room candidates. He even makes them laugh: several people have taken-themselves off the list—Not my Popla. He can't wait till the NR3 is opened up again so he can go inside and press that button that he thinks will erase his 'pain'. How does anyone really know if death is better? These children…" she shook her head. "Why are they so anxious to not exist? What makes matters worse is… my husband… his heart isn't very strong. Popla's death—if he tries again and succeeds—may mean his father's."

The Captain looked at her with a sad, measured interest, "No disrespect meant, your governorship," the Captain added, "but, if I were you, I think I would have refused to come."

"I mulled that thought over, but, you see, the Council ordered this investigation, and Jonas and I are the only ones who can find out if these "pirates" are using time travel as a way of stealing from the Past. Their meddling could mean the disappearance of everything. I sometimes wonder if my own existence will be wiped-out before my birth. Who knows what fate will have in store for us if thieves like Errlus keep tampering with the Past's resources. Someone has to do something and Jonas, well, somehow his project took precedence over my personal problems. Why?—I don't know. What good is sending someone to the time before the Earth became like a small sun? That angers me."

"The Council knows best, I'm told." The captain interjected to show empathy for her dilemma.

"I wonder. Blind men and women, that's what they are—as far as my family's needs are concerned—but the Council has been for centuries the only way this crowded world can balance its peoples' needs. You know, I could resign, leave with my husband and son for some warm paradise, but then who would do this job. I've trained other people for five years now, and I'm still not sure any of them know all that's entailed to manage a continent. Good people too, but it seems only experience can really train a person on certain things. Perhaps I'm being too particular."

The sailor whom the captain had sent away returned. "Your call has gone through, Captain."

"I'll be right there. Excuse me, Ms. Anderson. We'll be diving to look for the downed vessel soon. You better ready your equipment."

"Yes, I'll do that Captain." Andrea said through clenched teeth. She was beginning to hate taking orders. She was angry at the need for professionalism at this time when she should have been with her family. She was angry at herself for leaving them. She took her hands from the rails. They were white from the clasp she had had on the bar. She rubbed her palms till the color returned, then, she combed her whitening blonde hair with her fingers and walked to her cabin like a condemned woman.

CHAPTER 9

BEFORE THE EARTH CAUGHT FIRE

Marcus and Francis – New Time Travelers

The men for the job were before him. Jonas felt a twinge of envy as he stared at the two arduously selected candidates: Francis Benevieve and Marcus Struder. They were the most skilled at primitive methods of survival and their looks were not too different from the men in the pictures that were brought to the Present by previously sent, unmanned vessels. Francis was a bit taller, but his eyes had that tired look that most of the photos depicted: black hair and dark eyes were other traits that he shared with the inhabitants of the traumatic time before the world nearly blew itself apart. Marcus's hair was a shiny copper. A little bit of dirt rubbed into his hair, made him look exactly like one of the people depicted in a picture from that era.

Earth -
Before Spontaneous Combustion of Landfills

Cleanliness did not seem to be an important attribute to these people. According to taped conversations acquired through miniature robot-operated time vessels, water, especially clean water, was scarce, almost sacred. These people rubbed clay on their skin to clean themselves. Many of those who came close to qualifying for these positions, refused to apply for any further testing, dropped-out voluntarily, once they found out how filthy the living conditions would be.

These two had studied the language disks, the costumes, customs, mannerisms of the people, all the information available and still they exhibited no reservations to living in that time. Their wives knew the risks and supported them. They had good family backgrounds. They had peaceful temperaments, and they both took their responsibilities seriously. Jonas felt lucky to have found two men that qualified so well. They even liked one another which would help on their mission to find out how people managed to survive in a world that was nearly all fire. They would have to help each other survive in a toxic environment as well as gather the research needed.

The ship was ready. All the equipment was packed and placed in specified areas so as to keep the balance of the ship as it was designed. They entered the oily, egg-shaped vessel, waved goodbye, and then strapped themselves in as the solid gold panel was caulked into place with liquid metal. They listened as the technicians carefully oiled the door and weighed different angles of the ship as a last minute precaution. Then the ship started to spin. A special gas was emitted by a pressurized canister and they dozed as the spinning increased in speed. In an hour they would arrive at the year 3057, and their work would begin.

Camouflaging the time machine would be their first priority. Making contact with the people, collecting samples of art, music, and newspapers (if any) would take up the next two months of their lives. Then they would return to what would be for Jonas, the next day, and then the newly acquired information could be fed into the computer. Perhaps they would learn more about the will to live from those destitute paupers of history.

The expedition was the second phase of the "Save The Children" project adopted by the Council of Continents. It was another chance at abolishing the need for the Disintegration Chamber—the room where young adults went after signing up for suicide by vaporization. It was more than just an experiment in time travel to Jonas because of his daughter, Gwendolyn Doucet Montgomery. She was still on the list. This was a way to save her from herself. Bernard Hopkins had closed the Disintegration Chamber called NR3 but it would be open again if the young people who wanted to use it insisted upon their easy, clean, brief deaths. If the candidates for the chamber completed the "prerequisite" that Bernard had mandated—and Jonas knew his daughter could complete any project she attempted—then soon he might lose her forever and nothing would bring her back.

What were the reasons people killed themselves? It seemed the best way to find out how to instill the will to live was to find out why those who seemed to have nothing to live for wanted to survive. His goal was to find the reason for passion. It inspired him once before to legally appeal to break the Council's rule forbidding time travel. They had allowed it in Bernard's case. Now they had allowed it again.

One third of the world's young people had registered for the NR3. Why so many had no will to live seemed unfathomable. Disease was eradicated; hunger was no longer a problem. Everyone lived to be over 150 years old for over a century now. All jobless people were cared for by their families without any financial loss being evident. Leisure time was abundant. Why, then, were young people opting for death. Suicides had increased at such a rate that the Disintegration Chamber—or "Nothingness Room" as it came to be called—was rebuilt three times over the course of the past hundred years. It prevented the rash amount of overdose deaths. It cut down on the amount of slashed wrist attempts, and lessened the number of teenagers who attempted to jump from high buildings.

If Jonas could have known of his daughter's new found interest, he might not have seen the necessity for this new project to the time before the Earth became like a small sun. But he did not notice her interest and he was worried that the stall on her goal to end her life was temporary. To Jonas, the mission was necessary for her and for other families whose children did not want to live.

Being the director of the Time Cell Corporation allowed him the legal right to explore the unknown Past and he craved this more than sustenance, money, or power. It was almost an obsession to him as well as an obligation; but he was adamant about the rules. No one could stay in the Past for more than two months. No one could marry or copulate in the Past. No one could bring someone from the Past to the Present.

Bernard's case was an exception. He had been brought from 3040 years before the scheduled mission that saved him. He had been at the brink of death in a fire that consumed his home completely in the year 2059. These two reasons made his "abduction" allowable. His presence in their time had been planned for years before the time that Jonas and Andrea had first left to rescue him from the brink of his own death years ago. Several attempts failed and were retried to bring him from the past to the year 5090. No one had ever been brought from the Past before and no one was allowed to do so in the future due to the damage it might cause history. According to the Council of Continents, if a major change was caused by an explorer, another time vessel would have to go back and nullify the disturbance before its expected occurrence. Jonas followed their directives like a fanatic. Time travel was like a religion for him and like many strong beliefs, the solace it would bring would cost him dearly.

CHAPTER 10

INSIDE THE VOLCANO

The ship was now a small sliver of rusty brown that looked like a dash in the rippling murky green water above her. Andrea was taking samples of the ocean floor near some torn seaweed. Her element analyzer was vibrating as it calibrated the weight and size of an unusual stone she had found. She was surprised at the outcome. It was a substance unknown to her. It seemed to be a new element. She imagined it part of a meteor from a collision that occurred long-ago but she didn't see any craters. There were protrusions from the Earth's crust but not indentations. There was a huge volcano in back of her and thin volcano-like vents that released waves of heated water with a few bubbles. She had been down for twenty minutes. A group of scuba divers accompanied her and assisted her in finding unusual rocks and analyzing and recording their findings with their own element analyzers. There was no evidence of a ship wreck.

Andrea swam to the top of the volcano and looked in. The others looked at each other and nodded. One diver went to a seaweed bed and turned something in a clockwise motion. Andrea was unaware of their movements. They followed her to the top of the crater, 16-feet in diameter. She motioned to the two divers with the largest lights to circle down. They dove-in after briefly scanning the bottom. Andrea went next, the others followed. She descended in elongated spirals. The others, more familiar with the procedure, traveled at a steeper incline. She admired their sense of balance, their lack of vertigo. She took her time. At the bottom she saw what she was looking for: a thin, circular indentation in the sand.

Abduction!

She brushed away what she could and found the indentation to be a circular sheet of thick metal about 4 feet in diameter. She took out her camera and was about to take a picture when a net fell beside her. Other nets fell. A member of Andrea's team grabbed her by the arm while motioning to swim up. A slow moving harpoon appeared between her and the fellow diver trying to assist. The next net thrown entangled her so her diving crew grabbed part of the net to drag her with them up out of the volcano and towards the boat. Andrea could almost see the top of the volcano but the foreign scuba divers caught the other side of the weighted net and shot harpoon guns at those fleeing. Andrea noticed no one was hit even at such a close range. For a few seconds she thought it was all "staged". The last barrage of flying harpoon spears seemed to be a cue for her team

CATHERINE MARIE WEISS-CELLEY

to abandon her. She felt like a prize fish. Were they Errlus's pirates? Was that circular piece of sheet metal actually a hatchway into their headquarters? What did they capture people for? Were the harpoons just scare-tactics? It seemed they weren't aimed to kill.

She dropped her equipment in the net and took out a small knife. As they dragged her, she grabbed a side of the net and cut away the strands one at a time to make a hole wide enough for herself. They tugged the net toward a dark shadow among the rocks and went into it. It was a darkened entrance. She couldn't see anything. She heard a grinding hum of machinery, and then the lights were on and water was leaving what she then realized was an airlock. A few of the other divers ascended a ladder. One of the divers pushed her in the same direction and pointed for her to ascend. She climbed awkwardly since she was not used to the change in gravity. She concealed her knife in her palm as she climbed. At the top, she slid it under her wet suit while one of the divers folded the net.

"Hey, it's cut!" the diver yelled.

A woman wearing a darker suit than the others, reasoned with Andrea in a calm voice.

"The air lock is closed. There's no way out that you know of. Take the knife and slide it over toward me."

Andrea realized for the first time that she was a prisoner. She slid the knife from her sleeve, put it on the floor and pushed it toward the dark-suited leader.

"Thank you for being reasonable." Said the woman in charge as another diver picked up the sharp object. Then the dark-clad diver addressed another of her crew and told him to take Andrea to cell-block nine.

CHAPTER 11

EARLY RETURN:
A TIME DISRUPTION

Bernard at Gwen's Apartment

Something was different in the lab. Gwendolyn had come early to do research. Bernard had woken her last night when he had shut her door. It had been their ninth "date". They had tea and crumpets again but this time they talked more about Andrea than about Popla. Why was she abducted? First a whole ship in that area disappears and then Andrea is taken by force. How would this affect Popla who was still in a psych ward at the Hospital?

Always, when Bernard visited with Gwendolyn at her apartment, they talked for hours, and then he would offer to play the piano as he always did. It was becoming a tradition. Gwendolyn loved the music. It made so many memories come back to her.

She had gone with him to the Arts building where Bernard was assisting the NR3 candidates with their projects. Some of the candidates were preparing for a parade. Feathers and sequins were all over three of the huge outer rooms.

Somehow she imagined the workshop being where Andrea had been taken. She imagined Andrea dressing Popla in a bird costume and sending him off to swim in some sunlit field with fish. What a dream. She was surprised she fell asleep again. Bernard's music was like a drug to her or maybe it was just the late nights she would spend doing research at the lab. She was trying to find out more about Bernard's past, his wife, his sister.. As usual she went to the window to watch Bernard's cab drive away; then she washed, dressed, and headed for the lab to do more research on his plays and family.

She was somewhat alarmed to find the door open and the lights in the back "on". She figured her father, Jonas, was working early to ready for the return of the time travelers. She pushed the "on" button on her computer; then plugged in a search program for ancient drama. Instead of the normal "beep" sound, she heard a moan. She passed it off by telling herself she was hearing things because of tiredness, then she clicked on a small file that seemed appropriate since it was labeled "TWENTY-FIRST CENTURY PLAYS" She heard the moan again and then a scent unfamiliar to her reached her nostrils and caused her to cough and wheel around to find the source. Did a pipe break? she wondered. She smelt chemicals in the air—strong, putrid-smelling chemicals mixed with garlic, onions, or heavy perspiration. A whispered "help" barely audible, reached her ears. She spun around again expecting to see the words "help" flash on the screen, then she tip-toed to where the lights had been turned on since before her arrival. The scent grew stronger. She saw some mud and brown grass smudged on the floor, as if someone had walked to the public telephone at the back of the room. She saw an open directory and then heard a cough and a more audible whisper.

"Help me, please."

The voice was male and hoarse. She was afraid, ready to bolt for the door but compassion overwhelmed her. What if Errlus's men had broken in and hurt an employee. She walked closer to the sound and saw the time cell with its seared opening. It had arrived early.

Something's Different About the Lab

She looked inside and saw a dark-haired man who seemed familiar somehow. He was strapped to the chair. His hands were tied with ropes. He was the source of the smell. Tar-stained boots caked with mud and grass made the air inside the vessel almost unbearable. She held a kerchief to her nose. She knew this man now to be Francis Benevieve, one of the time travelers sent yesterday.

"Where's Marcus…? And why would your friend leave you here and not untie you?"

He coughed and cleared his throat so as to be able to speak. He seemed more drugged than hurt.

"He's gone to get Jonas. "He's no *friend*. A friend would have left me. Please, untie me. I've got to get away before he's back or…" Tears filled his eyes and he took in long breaths of stagnant air. "I'll never see her again."

"Who…? Why?" she asked. Questions bombarded her mind and answered themselves a dozen different ways.

"Mindy." He said. "I…" he seemed ashamed. "I loved her. We… were lovers. It's forbidden by the Council—I know, but— she…" He shook his head. "She's everything. Marcus brought me back by force, drugs. We stayed too long. I've got to get away and get back… somehow. Untie me, please." He looked passed her as if looking for a dreaded interruption. Then he pulled his wrists apart as much as possible. It seemed he would pull his hands off as he winced and screamed. "Ah, Mindolin! Don't be dead to me!"

"She heard me speak of a far-a-way world in the future with ships to carry them to a beautiful place. I told them of streams and mountains without smoke and they listened like children to a fairytale and Mindolyn fell in love… with me." He said incredulously. "Then Marcus tricked me with a drugged piece of meat and dragged me back to the time cell.—I've got to get back!" he said.

"Her hair was the color of night. Her skin…" He imagined breathing her scent and coughed violently. "Her skin has the scent of musk and tea leaves." He coughed again. "Not like this." He shook his head. He pulled at his wrists. "Please help me get away."

The First Night Francis Speaks

The Second Night Francis Speaks
The Shadows Talk

Third Night…Mindolyn Falls in Love

Gwendolyn looked in back of her to see if the way was clear, then she undid his seat belt and helped him slide to the floor. She started to undo his ropes as he stumbled against her toward the door.

"But how can you go back? That takes money. No one has that kind of money."

He then confirmed what she had been thinking all along.

"Errlus. I've got to find Errlus. Perhaps I can convince him, make it worth his while."

"Errlus…" she wondered to herself, that's who this man reminded her of."

"Is he a relation to you?"

The tall man smiled weakly. "I wish." He said "But no…. I have a friend who—I suspect—is a recruit. He's in another city, near the coast. It's a long shot but I've got to see her again. Life is nothing without her."

Gwendolyn knew the feeling. She missed her husband every day. Memories of him sometimes brought tears. Maybe Errlus could help her save him and her son from their deaths. Maybe it could be done, she thought, for the price of some harmless information. She started to believe that by helping this tall, dark-haired man get to Errlus, she would be helping her husband. She knew it was naïve to think so, but, it also would be disobeying her father and she relished this idea of getting back at him for not helping her go back in time to stop her son and husband from meeting with a fiery death. It was worth being ostracized from society by helping a disruptive time-traveler meet a criminal if her father was upset by it.

She was tired, but she could get him to the car and to a hotel, then bleach his hair, nurse his cuts, find out more of his plan and reasons and if it seemed too ludicrous or dangerous an idea, she could turn him in. Deep inside, she hoped his reasons were sane and his plan—possible; then, perhaps her own plan would be possible.

The cameras were taping their moves. Once out of the building they would be free of video observation but she would have to hide herself until the time she would be turning this fellow in or decoying attention from his endeavors.

The parking lot was still empty. She pointed to her company car and he hobbled to it. She unlocked and opened the passenger side. As she started the car and pulled-out onto the highway, he was looking at her with intense interest through swollen, squinted eyes.

"You're Jonas's daughter, aren't you?" he asked.

"Yes."

"Do you know my wife?" he asked.

"No." She had forgotten all time travelers had to be married so as to prevent what he apparently indulged in.

"I thought for a moment that might be why you were helping me." Every muscle in his body ached. He spoke as if in great pain. "Our marriage isn't one you see. Another man… I hid that from your father to do this… job. But why…?" He looked at her intensely trying to read her motives as the car's turns and swerves sent spasms of pain up-and-down his slouched spine and bruised ribs.

"Why help a stranger?" he asked with a trace of suspicion in his voice.

"My husband died.... I know what love is and what it's like to lose someone."

"Even if it means '—an end to the world as we know it.'?"

"Even then, besides, I feel—I don't know it for a fact—but I feel that the order of the world can't be changed by small meddlings in the Past. I believe there's some kind of pattern that prevents disastrous changes and that all the so-called 'disturbances' capable of being made are part of the entire pattern."

"I hope you're right, because if possible. I'm going to make some drastic changes."

"I will as well—if possible."

CHAPTER 12

OLIVIA

It was the same dream. The molten lava wall buried them. They were 12-feet apart this time, holding their arms out to each other before they disappeared. He heard the thunder and crackle of liquid rock moving. The ground moaned like a woman sometimes. He woke.

Errlus – Above the Molten Gold…Finds His Wife

"This tea will help you sleep—if that's what you want."

It was a child's voice. Or was it a woman's. The darkness of the room hid her identity. He didn't like surprises. "Who are you?" Errlus commanded in an almost angry voice.

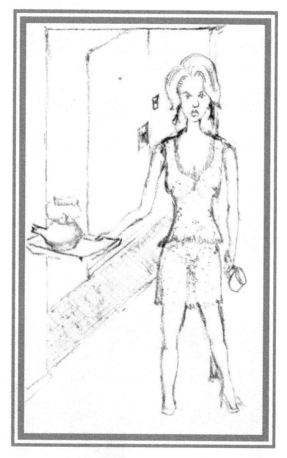

Seduction of Errlus

She was afraid to speak for a moment, afraid of being put out again like she was a few months ago when she had tried this while his wife was alive. Now his wife was dead. He had been without a woman for some months. She came from the shadow and handed the tea to him with both hands. She was shaking. "Olivia." She said timorously. Then she added in as sultry a voice as she could muster. "But names aren't important... Are they?"

He brought his hand up so fast; he knocked the cup from her hands. He grabbed her right wrist and held it so tight she couldn't move. Then he pulled her towards him, kicked the covers from around him and made her lie at his side. She was the 'lovesick puppy' he had put outside his room less than six months ago—when Johannah was alive. Now, his wife was gone and he was miserable. Perhaps this was what he needed.

He toyed with the buttons of her thin chiffon top. She looked at him with parted lips. She seemed afraid. He leaned over her and kissed her shoulder blade. A musky perfume intrigued him. He looked at her. She was more beautiful than anyone he had ever seen, even Johannah. Her pale blue eyes seemed like jewels, but something was missing, some calm glance he expected, some wise, understanding, peaceful look was not there. He wished it was his wife's face before him. With one hand he started to pull the rest of her thin, ruffled strap from her shoulder blade. She shuddered and let out a nervous breath. She watched his sad eyes focusing on the material as it slid towards her elbow and slowly almost undetectably, she tugged her arm free from the cloth. He kissed her neck as she pulled the rest of her clothing aside. He slid his hand along her breast, beneath her shoulder blade and up her back. Then he lifted her naked torso and pressed it against his own while they both lay on their sides. He could almost circle her waist with his hands. She moved like water beside him.

She couldn't believe her luck. He was touching her, kissing her. She felt the black hairs of his chest against her bare nipples. She kissed his chin and spread her legs for the first time in months. Her loins burned with expectation and he, she knew, would soothe the emptiness inside of her. One hand cupped her hip; the other smoothed her brow and hair. He touched her lips; then kissed them for the first time. She tasted mint upon his breath. He tasted wine. He kissed her again; then mounted her.

She smoothed the hairs on his chest as he looked down at her. She circled his nipples with her palms. He was in her. All that seed… the perfect man—she thought. She spread her legs wider. He went "in" and "out" and "in" again.

She was perfect, every angle, hour-glass build, firm, full breasts, tight buttocks, then, shapely legs, and she moved like water. It seemed she knew his movements and intent and did whatever he wished her to do.

He thought of Johannah and his movements quickened.

It hurt somewhat. Was he too big? She thought. Was she too small? She tried to open herself as much as possible and relax her muscles. He was moving so fast, her breath was forced out of her with each thrust as he seemed to press the bottom of her spine inside her. She put her hands up beside her face and closed her eyes. He came. Small pulses beat inside of her. He moved slower. She relaxed again. She felt him twitching inside of her and was aroused. He put his arm around her waist and rolled with her so she was on top of him. Her breasts were now positioned above his chest. His beard tickled her chin. She felt the limpness starting inside of her and it made her inner walls tingle… all that sperm beating against her womb and she was not fulfilled yet. He came out.

He knew she did not have an orgasm, but he rested until she kissed him on the neck, then his chest; then put his dwindling member in her mouth. He looked at her face while she mouthed him. Her eyes were like pearls he thought. Her face was perfect, smooth, not a wrinkle or blemish. Her cheeks were almost the same pale pink as her mouth, as it puckered and slid up-and-down. He wanted her again, but she stopped and lay down beside him. Her breasts pressed against the only pillow on the bed. Her head was turned away from him but her back seemed inviting. He lay on top of her and kissed the back of her right ear lobe. He pressed himself between her buttocks, between her thighs.

Sodomy, she thought; he wanted to sodomize her, she thought. Would it hurt? She wondered. She pressed her buttocks up against his belly and arched her back like a cat in heat. He leaned over her and cupped her breast and entered her vagina. They both imagined themselves to be two-four-legged animals mating. He had to hold himself in her due to the angle and she, more aroused than ever before, started writhing and shaking like a wind-blown tree. He felt her pulse around him. He held her and didn't let himself ejaculate, let her finish. Her arms were tired and weak from the effort. She slid to the pillow. He laid half on top of her and stroked her arms and hair slowly till she fell asleep. Then he turned her over, spread her legs and entered her again. Her eyelashes fluttered, and she smiled. He pounded her over and over again. She was limp, more relaxed, moistened and not as tight. He watched her fluttering lids and slight hand movements as he went "in" and "out" of her. She was graceful, even asleep. He wondered how many men had had her. Was she a whore? He mused. He didn't really care. She was there for him now. She made herself available. He would use her as much as she let herself be used. This wasn't love for him. Maybe for her. To him, she was just a pleasant distraction from his problems. He slid his hands beneath her buttocks and pressed her to him as he emptied himself in her once again.

CHAPTER 13

GWEN: IN HIDING

Gwendolyn had been up all night. It was three o'clock in the morning: 23 hours from the time she had found Francis drugged and tied in her father's lab. The hotel room to which she had brought him was now dark. Only the television screen lit the room. An old movie file was playing. It would keep her awake, she hoped, so she could monitor the progress of her patient. The morning before she had slept for only six hours but adrenaline kept her going. This time-travelling fugitive may offer her a chance to rescue her husband and son. That chance was worth a few hours of lost sleep. It was worth becoming a hunted criminal to the rest of her civilized world if she could get even one of them back.

Francis was feverish. At four in the afternoon, she had detected a fever and had gone to a nearby convenience store for supplies. He did not seem to be congested but he was shivering and slipping "in" and "out" of consciousness; so she bought some liquid aspirin, a cheap old-fashioned thermometer, a mud-mask to deter Francis from acquiring any physical interest in his care-taker, some toiletries, and two pairs of men's pajamas: one for him and one for herself. They fit her rather loosely but they presented a more modest appearance than the negligee provided by the hotel. She figured if she were to be alone with a man for a number of days, she could not risk enticing him. She even braided her hair and wound each plait around her ears to make herself look less attractive.

She was starting to put a mud mask on for the night when he stirred again. She gathered together the wet towels, thermometer, a glass of water, and the aspirin and then went to him.

It was 3:14 a.m. His next aspirin wasn't due till 4:45 but this dose would have to be early. His forehead was burning compared to her cool brow. She undid his top and put the thermometer under his arm. She tried to hold him still while he mumbled nonsensically in a dazed state; she was worried that he would dislodge the thermometer.

Three minutes passed. The thermometer read 103.6 auxiliary. That meant 104.6. She had to cool him down. She slipped a spoonful of liquid aspirin into his mouth and smoothed his throat so he would swallow, then she put a cool rag on his head and tried to wake him so he could bathe in cool water but he was delirious.

"No Mindy, no Mandy." He stammered. He was shivering. "It's too cold. I'm tired." He brushed her hands away.

She stood there wondering what to do next. She would have to call a doctor, authorities, but then, he might be recognized, then imprisoned and she would never have a chance to meet with Errlus and ask him to rescue her husband from a past death. She started to undo the rest of the buttons on his shirt. She took his right arm out and then brought the rag from his head to his neck and chest. He sat up and then she was in the air. He pulled her over his body, then under him, and straddled himself on top of her.

"You minx, I said it was too cold, but OK." Then he threw his shirt off and started to undo his pants. She screamed, "Francis, no, I'm—"

He hushed her with his hand partly in her mouth.

"Shhh, do you want Marcus to break in again. Then your father will have to break up the fight and all that time will be wasted."

She was scared. Was this really happening? She wondered. Was this animal really going to rape her while he was in a state of delirium? "Francis, please…"

"Ah, ah, ah, I love these noises you make but Shhh." He kissed her lips and undid the buttons near her neck; then he kissed away the shirt. "Mandolin…" he said over and over again.

Was he saying "Gwendolyn?" she thought. She closed her eyes and tried to imagine it was her husband. He unbuttoned the section of shirt covering her breasts and kissed her there, then another button came undone and another. With each undone button, he kissed her and said the name that sounded so much like her own. His voice was her husband's it seemed. Her shirt was completely open and he kissed her hips and he pulled away the elastic from her waist. He slid his hands down her thighs and pulled the pants off. She tried to roll away.

"Ah, you she-devil," he said, "always playing games."

He grabbed her waist and kissed her neck as he pulled her close and slid her panties to her knees, her back was flushed against his chest. He put his hands between her naked thighs and pressed the mound of hair there. He stuck his finger in.

"You're ready girl." He said and then he laid her down facing him while he slid his pajamas off one leg at a time, making sure his movements straddled hers.

She held her legs together. She *was* ready. She wanted sex but she didn't want it like this, without some form of love. She was nothing to him, she thought. He was nothing to her. She would not be able to handle the feelings afterwards. It would wreck her emotionally for a long time. She would feel cheap, like she had settled for just the physical, didn't wait for a spiritual mingling like she had had with her husband and hoped to have with Bernard.

He lay on top of her and tried to spread her legs with his own as he removed the rest of her clothes.

"Mindolyn" he said.

It sounded so much like her own name being spoken by her husband that she nearly parted her thighs. She felt him there throbbing between her legs. All she had to do was relax and he would press in, she thought. She had forgotten how good it could feel…, but NO, she thought. She wasn't ready. She could conceive if he… entered her, she thought. She had experienced the slight pains that meant she was close to ovulating. She started pushing him and screaming.

"No, NO! Francis. Stop! I'm Gwendolyn." She tried to pull his hair.

"Shhh, don't laugh so loud and Marcus won't bother us. Stop tickling." He laughed and tried to cover her mouth with one hand and hold her hands above her head with his other hand.

"Marry me, Mindy-Mandolin, marry me."

She imagined he was her husband for a second. He went in her pushing deeper. She felt herself tremble, wanting more of the sensation and feeling ashamed for wanting it.

He was saying, "Quiet now. Let's forget the world awhile." He was moving slow. His brows were lifted, losing himself inside of her. Two of his fingers were partially in her mouth, resting there after trying to quiet her. She bit him as hard as she could. He screamed and pulled away from her. He stood up and held his hand. She noticed sweat on his brow. The fever was breaking in more ways than one she thought. She scurried away from him to the floor on the other side of the bed. She was gasping. She wanted to cry and vomit at the same time. She pulled the sheet around her. All she had on was an unbuttoned pajama shirt. There was mud from her mud pack facial on his hand and his pillow, as well as her face. Slowly he realized what he must have done: that his dream was partly real. He grabbed his pajama bottoms from the floor and hid himself somewhat as he tried to apologize. She stifled him with a halting hand.

"You've been sick… understand? –Stay away! You've had a fever. I guess you were delirious. Please…, go get a cold shower. It will lower your fever and… take care of what else ails you."

He backed out of the room.

She put on her panties and pajama bottoms. Then she took two spoonfuls of aspirin and walked in toward the bathroom. The water was running. She yelled to him. "The medicine is on the dresser. In three hours time, you'll need more. You better keep taking it or I'll call the authorities."

She felt confused. Did she let this happen? Did she encourage this to happen? Who could she talk to? She would wait until he was done his shower and talk to him, if she could, but she fell asleep, and she did not hear him when he left.

When she awoke, the long shadows and bright lines of sunlight streaked the room like a jail cell. The quiet in the room made her realize she was alone. She slowly lifted her head from its uncomfortable position. Jail, she thought. That's where she would be once she was found. The daughter of a Time Cell executive put in prison for helping a fugitive who could have changed existence as they knew it. If she was pregnant from the "rape", she would be labeled this fugitive's lover. What could she do? The time she had now was her only free time. She would soon be found. Bernard, she thought; she could talk to him. She would call him. He could comfort her. She would even go as far as seducing him just to get rid of this dread she had of worrying that inside of her now, she may be carrying a fugitive's baby. Sure, it could be she wasn't pregnant at all but—if she was to be sent to prison somewhere, she wanted to be with child, with Bernard's child, so as to not be alone, so as to tolerate the dishonor with a diversion, so as to not feel such a victim of a rape. She called Bernard. Things were so different now; and she almost craved the difference. Did Francis rape that girl in the past? She did not know. She would just cherish whatever time she could steal before her arrest. Her father would never understand. That knowledge of her father's disapproval made her own disgrace tolerable. She wanted her father to be uncomfortable with his choices. She hoped Francis would meet Errlus. She hoped there was a Mindolyn from the past who would be saved. She no longer wanted to die.

The phone—Francis must have used the phone to call his contact. She picked up the receiver and hit the redial, wrote the number down. Later, she would call and set up her own "arrangement" with Errlus. Her knowledge of the Time Cell Corporation may entice him to assist her in rescuing her husband and son. She would wait till the time of her possible pregnancy was passed, then get her family back and leave her baby with either Bernard or her father. This hope kept her from the worry that hung like a tombstone above her head. She was surprised at her will to live, dizzy with the events of last night, almost happy that her father would soon realize how wrong he was not to help her before. She rose to shower-off the caked mudpack and dress in such a way that Bernard… could not refuse her.

CHAPTER 14

BEFORE THE DARII LANDS

The Darii Lands

Bernard was knocking on the motel room door. He had been over Dominick's when Gwendolyn had phoned. His service had transferred the call. That was 43 minutes ago. He had told Popla's father that he had to leave for an emergency, one of his students was in trouble. He didn't tell him who it was and hoped he hadn't recognized Gwendolyn's normally calm strong voice in the near hysterical state it, then, was in. Gwendolyn had spoken like a child, soft voiced, questioning, small gasps between the words. She seemed to have been crying.

What could have made her want to help a criminal escape? He wondered. Was she part of the "network" she had spoken of? Was that time disrupter actually a man she was in love with? If so, then why had she been so encouraging to his own timid advances? Bernard was beginning to think that their chance rendezvous were becoming more like dates. What made her so upset? If Francis were actually her love interest, did he leave her for someone else, was that why she was crying?

He knocked on the door again.

The knob turned and Gwendolyn opened the door a crack. She smiled nervously and let him in. Her hair was wrapped in a towel and she was wearing a terry-cloth robe provided by the linen service.

"Hi Bernard. Excuse me. I had to get a shower. Please, make yourself comfortable. I have tea simmering."

She looked disconcerted as she patted her hair and adjusted the collar on her robe like she didn't know what to do with her hands.

"I'll just be a minute or two. I just want to put on something more decent." She disappeared into the bathroom.

On the top of the table, there was a basket of rolls, crackers, butter and jelly. He bought out some plates and knives and poured the tea. He noticed the bed was neatly made but two pairs of pajamas were folded at the bottom of the mattress. He shook his head in dismay as he worried about her choice of a partner and her, now criminal, record. In a way, she was an accomplice to Francis Benevieve's crimes, because she had helped him escape.

She came out of the bathroom in a silk shirt with three-quarter length sleeves. Her skirt was a sleek navy blue corduroy that ended an inch below her knees with a four-inch slit between her legs in the "front" and the "back" to allow her mobility in such a narrow tube of material. Her hair was still wet. She was drying it with a towel. The scent of her shampoo was like a musky sandlewood.

"I poured the tea." Bernard said.

"Thank you, Bernard." She sat on the couch just four feet from the dining table and stared at the basket.

"I'm not hungry but help yourself."

She seemed hesitant to say anything. A tense silence loomed between them.

"Do you still feel like talking…? I'm not sure I can help you with— Perhaps a counselor or old acquaintance would be easier to confide in." He buttered two rolls, as he spoke and put one on a plate in her direction. She looked pale he thought. She seemed the type that forgot to eat when she was upset. Food helps the mind he thought to himself as he also subconsciously knew it would help fill the quiet between them.

"No… This is something—something I have to tell *you*. I wanted to tell you the other night but—"she was looking directly at him. "it seemed inappropriate.' She looked away and covered her face with her hand as if to awkwardly brush a strand of hair. "Still does." She was sitting sideways on the sofa and her right arm was positioned so as to support her chin. "Especially since, well, what happened—" Her hand was half covering her mouth as she spoke. She looked directly at the bed 10-feet away from her and just six-feet to the right of Bernard who stood facing her from behind the table. "—what happened… here. I wish I could know how you'll feel about me… once I tell you." She looked at him briefly, and then looked away.

Bernard tried to suppress the emotions welling-up inside of him. Jealousy and anger were things he knew he had no right to feel but somehow they seemed to be fighting to take over his calm. Still, he managed to sound sympathetic.

"I'm here to listen. I haven't called anyone about your location, but, as you've probably guessed, your father is devastated."

She cupped her head in her hands as she propped her elbows on the arm of the couch.

"He had told me he was in love—Francis, that is—that he had to get back to her no matter what. I had to help. It was like helping my husband somehow. Then the fever…."

She stood up and walked toward the window with her arms folded against her stomach.

"Fever?" Bernard said. "Are you ill?"

She felt her head. "No, I don't know." She said absentmindedly, almost mechanically. "I… don't care anymore. He was 103.6 degrees, actually: 104. I had to cool him down… cool cloth on his head. I started to undo his pajamas to wipe his chest with the cloth. He was delirious and he thought—acted like I was… her. Mindolin. It sounded so much like my own name. His voice sounded like my husband's once, when he had a cold. He held me there."

She was staring at the bed and rubbing her arms. Bernard was dumbfounded. He practically fell into the chair. "I tried to get away, but he was skilled. It was like he thought I was her, playing a game. He said, 'Let's forget the world awhile.' I found myself wanting to pretend it was my husband, but I wasn't using any protection. I didn't want to have this stranger's baby. What if he actually raped that girl in the Past—Mindolin or Mandolin as he sometimes called her— then he *would* be a criminal, not a man so in love he couldn't think about the rules. If so, I would have ruined my reputation, hurt my father, because of a foolish wish to meet Errlus like Francis had intended.

"You see…" she looked directly at Bernard hoping for understanding, "I wanted to go to Errlus—promise him anything… within reason, like Francis planned to—and ask Errlus to go back in time to stop my husband and son from burning in that accident."

Bernard was aghast. His mouth was open and his left foot seemed frozen in a "V" as he rested it on his heel with the tip of his shoe in mid-air. He had hardly breathed since she started talking and now he was out of breath, but he didn't want to seem breathless, so he got up and paced. He knew he should say something reassuring and compassionate, but he couldn't think of what to say, so he vocalized the first question he could think of.

"And where is he now?" he said. "Did his fever get so high during his delirium that he evaporated into a powder on the sheets or did he finish and exit for parts unknown immediately afterwards?"

He was surprised at how angry he sounded, how angry he felt. He put half his fist into his mouth and bit his knuckles as if he were trying to block anymore words from exiting.

"Bernard!" she said in the most vulnerable voice he had ever heard. "Don't be angry at me. I had to talk about this. There's..." she shrugged her shoulders and looked away as if glancing at all her prospective friends behind the walls of the building and in the city. "no one else... and I feel like... nothing.... Like I'm worth nothing. I was hoping, by telling someone, and you seemed the only person around that cared—by telling you, I could start to feel a sense of worth again, but, perhaps I shouldn't have even called you."

Bernard still had half a fist in his mouth. He lowered his hand while looking at the teeth marks he had made.

"I'm sorry." He wanted to walk toward her but he felt he didn't have the right.

"I spoke without thinking." He put his head down and ran his fingers over the smooth wooden back of the chair.

"I guess—"He smiled and looked at her briefly, then focused his eyes on the wood grain of the chair again. "I guess I was angry that someone could have treated a person as good-hearted (he thought of how often she visited Popla at the hospital), special (he thought of how she helped him organize his files of projects by the NR3 candidates), fine (he thought of how she always looked sophisticated and noble whenever he saw her) as you are..." he picked up his tea saucer and set it down to line-up with the basket of rolls at the center of the table, "—how someone could have treated you... like you... indicated—mentioned."

He was also jealous he thought, but he couldn't tell her that. He was ashamed of himself for wishing for a brief moment, that he had been this "Francis" character. He stared out the window afraid of being obvious with his mannerisms. He was afraid she would detect his unsteady breath and movement and take it for what it was: lust, mingled with a kind of puppy-love he hadn't felt for years. She did not need another intrusion on her values and emotions he thought.

"Bernard, do you know what will happen to me when I am caught—when I turn myself in, I mean."

"I have an idea." He said while still looking out the window." He pushed one of the vertically scalloped mini-blind slats with his hand to look at the traffic below. "I guess—prison: a few years maybe. Can your father do anything to lessen your sentence?"

"Yes, I probably won't even see prison. He'll just send me away to my aunt's in the Darii country, indefinitely. I may never be allowed in a country with a Time Cell Corporation in it. He is pretty strict about rules on time travel. I've been thinking prison would be easier than being forbidden to continue my career. Prison would be over with when I got out. Five years at the most, but at my aunt's… with no present skill adaptable to that region…. I would be starting all over again… like a child. I don't even know the language yet." She moved to the table and stirred some cold tea while looking at Bernard. She took a sip.

"While looking up information about you, I came upon a phrase you may have heard, 'It's okay to visit, but I wouldn't want to live there.' Darii-land: It's so alien from what I know. It would be lonely."

"Is that why you haven't gone to a doctor, you don't want to be turned in? You want to hold off on going to the Darii land?"

"Yes, partly and…" she looked at his wavy silver hair and felt her face flush, "and… Bernard, the other night when I met you outside the hospital…"

"Yes … oh." He said as if just realizing something. "Would you like for me to help you to see that fellow you had dinner with when I *first* met you at the hospital that time, before you call your father?"

"No." she looked at him directly as he stared back waiting for her response. She looked a little frightened again, he thought.

"I actually did not have dinner with anyone that night. I was hoping to *meet* someone that night."

Bernard thought of the small town bars he used to frequent. They were always filled with lonely, well-dressed women. He was surprised that Gwendolyn, who seemed too beautiful to be lonely, had dressed in the multi-faceted cocktail dress so as to have an encounter at one of the dives he imagined.

"What are you saying Gwendolyn?" Bernard asked almost afraid of the answer. He didn't want to hear her say she had wanted to be taken advantage of that night, and that, now, she felt cheap because she had, in a sordid way, gotten what she then wanted.

"Do you realize that each time I went to the hospital to visit Popla I knew *you* would be there, Bernard? Each time, I was *hoping* "you" would come home with me as you did sometimes for tea; and I wanted "us"... to be *more* than friends." She was not looking at him now. She was looking down at the rug, away from him so he couldn't see her face. "I've fantasized about us for some months now. I-I think I'm in love with you and I don't want to go away without ever feeling you close to me." She still could not look at him. "I hope you don't feel I'm tainted somehow because of what happened." She glanced at him, then away, quickly. He had a peculiar expression on his face.

"I bit him, Bernard... on the hand..." Bernard looked at his own hand which he had bitten himself so as to keep from saying something stupid. "I bit him to stop him from... pressing in. He didn't finish what he started. I felt him there and he made me want the sensation, but, not with him, If he were my husband... or you." She looked at him with a worried, vulnerable expression on her face. "If he had been you, Bernard," she started to cry. "I wouldn't feel so cheap right now."

He went to her and held her as she cried onto his shoulder.

"I wish things could be different. I imagined having your baby, being married again, taking care of you—and now, I'm going to be sent away because I had to try for my husband one more time." She held him as he held her. "You deserve so much Bernard. You have been through more trauma than most people can endure and you've come through it still loving people and accepting yourself. I love you, Bernard." She nuzzled her nose beneath his ear. "Make love to me, please." She whispered; then rested her head on his shoulder. "If I am going to have a baby because of this… incident, I'd like to think it's yours. I could tolerate that loneliness in my aunt's homeland more. I could love the baby more."

"Shouldn't you go to a doctor first? Maybe they could prevent such a pregnancy."

"No. I fell asleep after I bit him. Conception could have already occurred. I was tired, confused. He got a shower… and left, besides…" she looked away. "—all the doctors I could have trusted are friends of my father's. I would be caught without a chance of seeing you again."

"I could visit this Darii land."

"No." she smiled as her sad eyes focused on him. "No, there's too much here for you to do, too many people to worry about here. They need you, I guess, even more, than I do. You couldn't or just wouldn't go there because—"she moved away and walked to a box of tissues to dry her eyes.

I know I'm attractive Bernard, but… I'm basically a cold person. When it comes to making advances, I hold back. Deep inside, I don't feel attractive. I feel-funny looking, awkward. I think I must know somewhat how you must have felt with the disease you once had. I guess you also don't make advances often because of this odd image one gets of oneself at times." She went to him with her hands behind her back. Her hair was almost totally dry now. It hung in long, strawberry-blonde waves, framing her face. Her green eyes caught the light of the sun streaming through the slats of the shade and her cheeks seemed pinker than usual. Her lips were pale, almost lighter than her skin. Without thinking he touched her lips; he wanted to feel the texture of the rose petals they seemed to be at that moment. He combed the hair on the right side of her face behind her with his fingers and he traced the small loop of gold on her lobe. He kissed her there. She closed her eyes and parted her lips. Her hair had the scent of musk and wild flowers. He slid his left arm around her waist and kissed her on her cool lips that seemed as soft and moist as dew glistened petals. He slid his arm up to the center of her back and became more aroused as he realized she was wearing nothing but her shirt above his hand. He bent down and lifted her knees so that her feet were off the floor. She was lighter than he thought she would be. She caressed his neck with her left hand as he carried her to the bed. He put her there gently and brushed her cheek with his as he crossed to the window and shut the shades. He started to undress.

He heard her rustling the covers as she did her own undressing. He couldn't see her without the window's light striping the room as it had. He moved toward the bed and bumped his knee into the end table.

"Ow!" he moaned as she giggled.

"Perhaps this is an omen. Are you sure you want to do this, Gwendolyn?" he said.

"I love you Bernard. Don't back out now." Came her reply in a timorous, sultry voice.

He found the bed and seated himself beside her. She pressed her bare breast against his back as she massaged his chest and thighs and he then eased her down so her back was aligned with the bed.

He was on top of her, flushed against every curve of her front torso and legs. She felt his warm, soft flesh between her thighs, the curly hair of his chest against her nipples. He outlined the outer perimeter of her thighs with his hands, then circled her knees and slid his fingers up the inside of her legs toward his genitalia lying before hers. She parted her legs and felt him pressing. She looked at him and he at her. She loved his kind face. He had a sensuous mouth. It was the first time in years that either of them had willingly indulged in this experience. He penetrated the outer rim of her slowly as if venerating, memorizing a sacred moment.

She was moist and he moved slow so as to revel in the texture. She moved with him. He fit so well. She wrapped her legs around him. He pulsed and stopped to stall, too soon, an ending. After a few seconds, she moved, tightening her muscles and pulling, relaxing and pushing with a slow rhythm. He tried to think of something else for some moments. The movement was so stimulating he was almost too aroused. He thought of diamonds. She thought of seeds splitting into each other, pounding each other. She wanted him to reach the height of their movements just as she felt the tingling sensation start in her. She tightened and pulled and relaxed and pushed at a quicker pace. She felt him pressing into her womb and felt a pleasant burning sensation, then a quiver started and she felt deep inside of her the tremulous rhythm she longed for. She imagined the tiny sperm entering her and beating against the cell that would soon be a baby. He watched her writhe in ecstasy and felt her open even more as he pushed in and out. He let go of all his reserve and pulsed into her, back and forth, warm liquid caressing him, creating someone there inside of her, perhaps, he wondered and hoped. He thought of waves of music as their motions came together. They held each other like two people desperate to make the small time left to their love making last a lifetime in memories. They knew they had only a few days more and then they would probably rarely, perhaps never, see each other again.

Bernard wondered: *"Could he be a father?" "Would a child of his have his tumorous affliction?" "Could they cure it before the child even had a lump, since medicine was so advanced at this time?"*

He laid on top of her awhile, still inside of her. Then he moved to her side a little so as to not rest too much of his weight on her rib cage. She smiled at him. They were still joined limply, but comfortably below their waists. They dozed for some minutes. She woke first and kissed him awake and they started again. She thought of his music that first night she heard him play for the NR3 candidates. It was so powerfully played. It invoked memories in her that were long buried in grief: pleasant forgotten memories. She loved Bernard for this. He was so easy to love.

Images: Memories of Bernard's Music

Soon Bernard would have to see his students again and Gwendolyn would have to subject herself to the law, be prosecuted for aiding the escape of a prisoner. First, of course, she would try that number Francis had called to see if she could contact Errlus. She still hoped to rescue her family from their collision with the fuel carrier but if that proved fruitless. She would indulge herself with Bernard's attentions for as long as possible. She could stay in the hotel for a few weeks but pride would drive her to face her father, and the punishment he would have to give her.

CHAPTER 15

BARGAINING CHIPS

Apprehension was not something he was used to experi-encing, but after Johannah died, it plagued him and caused him to hesitate too often in his decisions. Before, he could have talked to her, but now, there was no one but himself. Everyone else did not know enough or he could not trust them enough to cover all the variables necessary. He had trusted Johannah. She was his conscience. She could quell any emotion he had in a way he could respect or revel in experiencing but she was gone and his indecision caused by not having her there to confirm or disagree with his opinion caused him to be angry, angry at himself and short-tempered with many of the people he commanded, especially Olivia. He treated her like a slave. Commanded her to get his food, his clothes; treated her roughly in bed, told her what to wear, to not wear; criticized her every move. She was perfect in form and grace but she was not Johannah and he resented her for that.

He walked to the picture over his desk. It was colorful, a gift from his mother, a painting of the town he was from so many years ago. He was 17 when he left. Did his father grieve for very long he wondered? He remembered how much his father worried about him if he took too long to go to the store. He remembered how his father had cried when he had thought the boy who died on the camping trip was his first born son. He sometimes hated being the oldest then. Sometimes he had to baby-sit for his younger brothers and sister. He wondered how their lives had been. So many questions and no time to find the answers that were buried in centuries and time travel. He remembered what his mother had said about how hard it was in the beginning: a new land, a new world; and his father, she told him, "was the reason they all are living so well". Everyone owed their lives to him. He brought them there where they could breathe clean air for the first time in their lives, where the water didn't have to be boiled, where disease seemed to cure itself. His father was regarded as a savior. He remembered how some people bowed to him as he passed. He remembered his friends asking him where his father had come from but he knew almost as little as they did.

Some People Even Bowed to Him

Once, when he was 11, he woke up late at night and saw his father and mother outside. They were looking up at the sky saying

"There's Earth." And his father looked worried. "Were we wrong Mindy? He said. She just kissed him and said "You've made 375 families happier and healthier. If you were wrong, at least it was for the right reasons." Then his father said, "But how many lives did I change for the worse or prevent? Did I change my own future? Will this all disappear?" His mother just put her arms around his father and said, "Let's walk. Let's walk and enjoy what we have now. Sometimes, by wondering if it all will disappear, you can lose it more while it's still here." And they walked into the warm Spring night air, arm in arm, passed all the wooden cottages, the little rounded bridge by the stream that led into the woods. They were gone till the early morning he remembered. His mother had pieces of leaves in her hair and looked radiant. They were so much in love.

Less than six years later he would disappear from their lives forever. He opened a drawer in his desk and took out a letter. It would explain things. It might ease the burden of their loss. Hopefully it wouldn't tell too much. He wished Johannah, his wise, witty, life-loving wife was there, wished he could wonder aloud with her, but it was his decision. No one else could help him weigh the pros and cons.

A knock at the door interrupted his concentration. He shut the drawer that held the letter to his father.

"Come in." he said.

A soldier walked in. "She read the book sir. She's getting testy. Hitting the walls of her cell with her fists. She broke a chair, sir. She wants to speak to her 'captors'. Perhaps it's time."

Errlus looked at the man sternly, measuring what he said.

"I had this scheduled for tomorrow but… there's no need to stall. Bring her to me Jason. And tell Mr. Benevieve I'll meet with him today not tomorrow as well… in the next room… 15 minutes from now." The soldier saluted and left.

Errlus pulled out the bible from his desk and set it on the table. A necessary prop and an ancient relic in one. History…. He wondered what his future would bring. It seemed so dark and empty without his wife, his son. What would the bible of his future hold for his family? Would he have a family? "All I need is the right men, the right women…." He thought to himself. He looked at the picture his mother painted of what seemed a three-mooned world. Johannah died on one of those moons. "We'll be coming for you Johannah." He said aloud.

"You talking to yourself Errlus?" came a cold-toned voice behind him. He swung around to see Andrea with the soldier he had just instructed a few minutes before.

Errlus smiled as if accepting a criticism from a misinformed friend. He gestured to the Bible and spoke with conviction. "There is a saying in our bible. 'Great men echo their own thoughts'. Many people I've met have called me great. I try not to let them down. Sit down Ms. Anderson."

Andrea stood. The soldier motioned her to the chair, but Andrea ignored him. She spoke angrily.

"What kind of bargaining chip am I to you? Why am I a prisoner here?

Errlus sat down, motioned to Jason to leave. As the door shut. He said "You are not just a bargaining chip your governorship. You are more valuable than that but your anger leads me to believe you are not ready to know."

"I have a right to know why you've stopped me from my work. My family needs me. My husband… may die if he's told of my disappearance… his heart…. I'll give you whatever amount you want. I have money, friends with influence. Name a price." She said this craftily, hoping to flush out his reasons so as to then deal with them. There were certain things she would die before forfeiting but money was not one of them.

"That's not what I want from you Madame. Besides, if your husband dies—with the money and connections you have, you can go back—or send someone back—to change that; can you not?"

Andrea's eyes narrowed. She was angry at having the possibility of her husband's death being talked about so lightly and she was angry at the disregard this man apparently had for a directive she was taught to die for.

"You know this is against a law that threatens everyone's existence…?" She said half questioningly while staring at his face to read any surprise or defiance and found that he seemed to be holding something back. "…but that doesn't bother you. You have done it though, haven't you?" she said incredulously. She finally knew the answer to the question that had plagued her for decades. Errlus was using time travel, perhaps even robbing the "Past" and "Future" as he did the "Present".

Errlus knew this to be a sensational subject to Andrea so it had to be explained even though it seemed odd that the reasons for using time travel weren't obvious to someone at Andrea's political level. He would have to let Andrea know what only his wife knew and a few people in his Informational Science Agency. In some way, it would be a relief to tell someone else. In addition to trying to enlist Andrea's assistance as a governor, he was hoping for an ally. Andrea was a good prospect.

"When I was 17, I had my first ride in my father's time pod. I disappeared from my family to arrive 1, 623 years later; but, you see, due to my father's influence—he was as you are: a leader of a…'continent'—there were people waiting for me. They taught and trained me and decided I should stay in that time rather than go back to the time when I disappeared from everyone I knew. They believed I was the catalyst to their existence. Not until recently, have I come to believe them… and due to the other studies I have conducted, authorized, I have come to believe that the patterns I find myself in and that I continue to maintain, are the reasons for the present day's continuation of… society. Everything you know that exists today, would not be there, if it wasn't for me."

"Whose 'society' are you talking about, Errlus?" Andrea said exasperatedly. Tired of what seemed a madman's ranting.

"Everyone's" Errlus said sadly and assuredly.

"Everyone in this time we now share." Errlus said as he turned to look at a picture his mother had left him, a view from his home town. There were what seemed to be two suns in a brilliant sky. They were actually moons. One was extremely bright and round. One moon was pale and crescent-like. A ghost of a third shape was slightly to the mid-left of the scene.

Scene from Errlus's Childhood Home

Andrea's exasperation turned briefly to fear. Was this menace to society more a crazy person than a thief? Errlus seemed strangely tired, almost off-guard for a moment. Andrea felt she could walk out since Errlus had his back to her but there was probably a guard posted and being in the middle of the ocean was intimidating, plus, she was becoming increasingly curious.

"Notice the two round sun-like objects on the left side." Errlus said while still looking at the picture.

Andrea looked at the unusual image printed on a crystal framed picture "Yes, an artist's error?" she said as unconcerned as possible.

"No. It's an attempt at realism that went quite well. You see— please sit down," Errlus said motioning toward a chair and tapping a bible on his desk. He had purposely planted a similar bible in her cell and he knew she had read it. He figured it may intrigue her curiosity since it referred to him. He knew he could not get her to help him by blind faith like so many people he had encountered but all he needed was her interest; then he could influence her. "—you see, I was born not long after this world nearly exploded.

"My father used spaceships to take us to a moon not far from Earth. He had readied it for our arrival through the use of time cells. Scientists whom he employed through the help of… someone in our present… changed the atmosphere of a then dead planet so as to accommodate life. It took several hundred years but it worked. This is a painting of that planet. Do you see the oblong, crescent-like shape here?" He motioned to the odd shape on the canvas.

"Yes." She said while half wondering if Errlus should be hospitalized somehow.

Errlus continued. "That's actually a moon covered with volcanoes erupting almost constantly. This is a painting of Ganymede done by my mother who is from Earth—from just before the time of the Dark Age. I have reason to believe that you also are a descendant of one of the 375 families brought to Ganymede from the burning Earth in the year 3057. In fact, when this Earth exploded so many centuries ago, there was not much chance of survival anywhere on that surface. Certain valleys in dense mountain ranges, certain islands, small underground civilizations that did not suffer much from the tremors, these places held only a few hundred families. Actually: twelve hundred and fifty-two families to be exact. That's how many groups of people there were in the settlements we found when we went back after things calmed down 2000 years later." Errlus looked at Andrea's expression which was filled with concern as if listening to a madman in a therapy session. Errlus figured this to be good since at least she listened enough to perhaps be influenced.

"I studied for 7 years after I arrived in the year 3623… of that world. A special school of teachers had been set up through the centuries to train subsequent teachers who would eventually teach me about space travel, history, geology, diseases from radiation, things I would need to know. Technicians were trained also to pass on the study of the time-cell I traveled in since then it was the last functional one left us. The leaders of that time—those times—had been instructed by… their first benefactor… that it was not wise to send many time cells throughout history. These men thought a great deal like your friend Jonas. Perhaps, each person in his or her own way is correct in reasoning the rules that were set down."

"Benefactor?" Andrea caught the word which triggered an alarm in her head. "And who was this benefactor?" She was worried that some group of people in a Corporation from a different time was the guiding force behind this madman's piracies.

Errlus looked at her through squinted eyes as if trying to read her mind. Her thoughts were so different from his own that he could only rely on body language and expression to guess her anxiety.

"I am this benefactor Mrs. Anderson. I am." Errlus said with a sad smile on his bearded face, tears beginning in his eyes. "My father—due to his wanting to save a woman from the Past, a time he was sent to by your friend Jonas, a Past time that existed just a few years before the Dark Age enveloped the Earth—my father formulated the plans for the existence of the Earth as it is today.

"Now, Mrs. Anderson, please sit and watch that wall to the left of the painting." He dimmed the lights and went to the door to the left of where he indicated. "There are two guards outside each door. Do not try anything, but notice the man in the room I am about to enter."

As the lights had dimmed, the wall became almost completely invisible—it must have been made of a special glass. She then noticed a dark-haired disheveled-looking man sitting in the next room He stood up to greet Errlus as Errlus entered from where Andrea remained as a captive spectator.

"Ah, Mr. Benevieve. I've been told you have great news for me."

"Errlus… yes… I do. There are mineral deposits you may be interested in… acquiring. Rare minerals, crystals, oil. I believe they'll bring great wealth to your cause and the odd thing about them is… no one owns them. They are there for the taking. All you need is some well-equipped time cells and… they're yours." He felt like a carnival huckster. He thought of Mindolyn and closed his eyes. "But there is a price."

"Always." Errlus replied. "Please sit down Mr. Benevieve. You look very tired. Let me get you some refreshments. Francis Benevieve started to refuse but Errlus insisted, "Actually, I have not had lunch." He hit a button on his desk. "Olivia!" he said in a harsh voice. "Bring in some sandwiches, juice and tea. And be quick." He looked at Francis and smiled. "Now what kind of proposition do you have for me?"

Andrea was surprised at the change. She was witnessing Errlus as he was making a deal with a man strangely familiar. Then it dawned on her who the man was: "Francis Benevieve", one of the men Jonas had sent back to the Dark Age to investigate the Past. Francis was back and somehow was turning traitorous. Andrea tried to listen intently. Then Olivia walked into the room. "Andrea!" she said in a startled voice. She held a tray and tried to hide herself briefly. She seemed embarrassed. Andrea noticed that Olivia was with child. She was still as beautiful as she remembered her but now Olivia was very tired looking and at least five months pregnant.

Andrea vehemently loathed Olivia because of how Olivia treated her son, Popla, Andrea and Dominick's only son. Popla had tried to commit suicide partly because of Olivia. Olivia had left Popla after having their unborn child stored in a cryogenic bank. She did not want to be a mother then. Her leaving broke Popla's heart. Then when the cryogenic bank burned to the ground, Popla overdosed on sleeping pills. Andrea blamed Olivia.

"Olivia…" Andrea said as coldly as possible. "What are you doing here?"

"I'm to bring refreshments for you, Errlus and Mr. Benevieve. Normally the kitchen clerks do this but, for some reason," she paused and frowned, "I was told to serve these lunches." She set the tray on the table. She knew Andrea was angry at how she treated Popla.

"How is Popla?" she asked without looking at Andrea.

"I don't know. He had attempted suicide just before I left for this mission I was abducted from. He has never gotten over you… or the loss of that baby you both could have had…"

Olivia instinctively held her stomach where the baby seemed to kick. Tears formed in her eyes at the thought of Popla being so hurt. She remembered how much he loved her. She missed feeling loved.

"I wasn't ready then, for a baby. I was 21. The cryogenic lab seemed the best alternative. He may be able to find a host mother—"

"The embryo lab burned to the ground a year ago. Your baby's dead." Andrea said coldly as if it didn't matter now to her.

Olivia felt the baby inside her kick again. She had to lean on the desk a moment. Andrea noticed this but went on in the same manner.

"So, whose baby is this you decided not to freeze. Did you get your pirate?" She looked at Errlus in the next room.

"Yes," she said then looked down to the tray. "…and no. I have to bring him his lunch." She went to the door then turned to face Andrea just before it. "I know you must think I'm some cheap… whore." She could hardly say the word. "…who took advantage of your son but, Andrea, I did love him then and not for his family or inheritance. He was sweet, innocent, kind…." She said this as if she missed those things and would never see them again." I thought love was a temporary feeling that had to be fully felt and when that stopped with Popla, I had to leave. Maybe I was wrong."

"When I called you in France and asked you to come back for him because he was suicidal, why didn't you come?"

"I never made it to France." She said sternly. "My ship was intercepted halfway there. "The person you talked to was a cover for my disappearance. I signed-up as a member of Errlus's group. When his wife died, I became—"she suddenly felt nausea rise inside her but stifled it. "—more than that." She looked away feeling a little ashamed. Andrea noticed this and could not believe it. Was she trying to act like a martyr?

"You had been following him for months. Don't make it sound like he raped you." Andrea said angrily.

"Oh, he didn't rape me. I seduced him…. But" she changed her tone and smiled defiantly at Andrea. "—be happy Andrea" she said sarcastically. "—I'm like Popla was when I left. I know what it's like to love someone who cannot love you back. Errlus… never loved me. He's just using me…. I guess, like I used Popla. He was there and interesting. I was—there. It's not enough… you know? I'm sorry Andrea for hurting Popla like I did but I really thought he felt as unattached as I did."

She grabbed the tray and walked timidly back to the door. "I wish I could go back." She looked Andrea in the eyes and mustered a small semblance of pride to say again: "I'm sorry. I wish things were different. Goodbye Andrea." Then she walked out.

A few minutes later she was in the next room with a tray of food and tea for Errlus.

Errlus was visibly annoyed.

"What took you so long? The tea is probably cold."

"No Errlus. It was on a burner out on the cart."

"So now it's brewed too strong." He said curtly. "You forgot the juice. Go get it." She left.

Errlus looked at the closed door, then, at Francis who seemed to be trying to ignore the outburst. "Pretty, isn't she?" Errlus said to Francis. He was also speaking for Andrea's benefit. He knew the connection between Andrea's son, Popla, and Olivia. Olivia could be a bargaining chip if all went well.

"Beautiful." Francis said half-heartedly. He was thinking of Mindolyn now three months pregnant or dead—depending on whether he could go back in time to save her.

"Found her in my room one night a year-and-a-half ago. Put her out as soon as I saw her there, the impudent home wrecker. Then my wife died." Errlus frowned. "A few months later she snuck into my room again. She's not my wife." He said somewhat angrily. "But she's a diversion. She'll do for awhile… till I can get my wife back."

Francis was intrigued. How did Errlus plan to rescue his wife from death? "What happened?" he asked.

Andrea leaned forward from where she was sitting to listen since Errlus's voice had gotten lower. Just then Olivia rushed in crying.

"Excuse me Andrea. I was heading for the kitchen then I realized I left extra juice in here. Excuse me." She grabbed the juice and rushed out.

Andrea heard Errlus say, "A wall of lava hit her and my son. I—" Olivia opened the door. She had composed herself but her voice was still shaky and her face wet with tears. "I brought the juice. Sorry it took—"

Errlus interrupted her. He was visibly annoyed for two reasons.

"Saying sorry is all you do well." He said disgustedly. "Put the thing down and get out." Olivia dropped one carton on the table and threw the other one at Errlus. It hit his shoulder.

"I wish you died with your wife." She screamed then ran out.

He looked after her, then at Francis. He smiled and sat down and lamentably said, "I did."

Francis knew right away what he meant but Errlus went on to explain for his benefit—and Andrea's who he knew was listening intently in the next room. He figured the anger he portrayed against Olivia might make Andrea arrive at a plan he had already conceived. Olivia could go back to Popla—in return for Andrea's assistance in finding and recruiting people to save his family. Once she worked with him on one or two missions—then—she would be on his side. With her leadership skills, he could leave the encampments he set up and head for ten years into the future, to further secure the settlements which now seemed just begun.

"You see, Mr. Benevieve. Do you mind if I call you Francis?"

"No. No, I-I don't mind."

Before a Wall of Lava

"Well, Francis, when that wall of lava hit my son, I froze and then I was hit by the same wall. At least that's what Jason tells me. He was there. He left afterward in the time cell on the hill. Later, he came back in another time cell and just before the lava wall that had hit me. He sprayed a narcotic on me that immobilized me enough to *"rescue"* me. I wasn't about to leave without them, and he knew that so he resorted to chemicals. Now, I find whenever I go back to that place and time, I feel like I'm fading. A friend with me said I was actually fading; so, I need volunteers to rescue my wife and son. I cannot do it. Jason is too valuable to risk. I am screening people now.

"I'll go—" said Francis, "if you'll—"

Errlus cut him off, "No, You will not go. There is reason to believe these mineral deposits you spoke of will supply some settlements we are now developing. What is your plan, Francis?"

Francis began telling Errlus of the gold in valleys that were filled with poisonous gases. Quartz in the sides of nearby mountains. Oil in a pool 20 miles from his home in the Past world. Then he told him his price. He wanted Errlus to rescue Mindolyn's family and possibly all of the people on the mountain with her family. "Of course, it is illegal to attempt changing the Past in this way according to the Council in charge of time travel." Francis said this in a voice that bordered on rage—then he changed his tone to his normal sense of urgency. "—but I have to change it. I can't let her die. She's… with child." Errlus gripped the armrest of the chair he was sitting on tighter, tried not to show any emotion; but Andrea, in the next room, noticed his sudden tenseness.

"Only three months if we're figuring correctly. I managed to hide the ship—time ship—from Marcus, my partner, so as to allow me to get to know Mindolyn more. She's amazing. I never knew love like this. –Read about it in old books but today, marriage, dating seems such a game. Life does not depend on who you marry as it does there. I feel honored that her father accepted me. Then Marcus drugged me and brought me back. I'd rather go back to die with her in her time than be forced to live in this time. But I figure… if I have a chance to be with her in all that misery, maybe I can stretch that chance a little further and have her rescued from it." He looked at Errlus and tried his sales pitch again. "There is great wealth in the resources there Errlus. All I'm asking is a Time ship or two to take her to one of your hideaways at present. These tremendously industrious people—they can help with the—"Errlus cut him short.

"Pregnant women cannot time travel." He said sternly. "They miscarry." Andrea in the next room said aloud to herself, "How does he know?" in astonishment and anger." She started pacing the floor as the magnitude of Errlus's operation seemed to grow before her eyes. "Why does he care?" She knew the answer could be a weapon against Errlus if she could find out why. She listened intently.

"B-But…" stammered Francis. "I'll go back first." His mind was racing. "To be with her—to ready the mining expeditions." He said quickly, conscious of the need to keep Errlus's interest. "We'll wait till the baby's born. Seven months. That should be enough time to set-up several mining camps."

"You'll risk your baby's life in a poisonous world?" Errlus said. "Mining would further endanger your family." He said cautiously.

Why does Errlus care? Andrea wondered. Why did this normally cold methodical pirate who kidnapped hundreds of people— why did he care about a crazy-man's love affair?

"It's all I have to pay you. The money here... belongs to my wife of this time, and it's not much... besides... I have no access to it now. We could set the return vessel to after the time the baby's born then start the—"

"Space travel, Francis" Errlus said slowly and deliberately as he looked directly at his listener. "has proven to be quite safe for young fetuses. On a new world, you'll need others to help. We can make arrangements for everyone on that mountaintop, possibly more."

"Space travel?" Francis stood up. "You've done that!?" He said incredulously. "Do you mean that we stay in space till the land is ready; or—". Errlus cut him off.

Just Before the Earth Became a Small Sun

"There are developments on a nearby moon in that time about 12 days from Earth. Would you be willing to live there?"

The smile on Francis's face grew from a wry grin to a point where his eyes twinkled. Something seemed familiar to Andrea about Francis then, but she could not place just what.

"Errlus," Francis said. "You're an amazing man. It's a deal." He reached his hand out to his. Errlus shook Francis's hand a long time realizing for the first time without a doubt who actually stood before him. This man was not a distant relative, not just a future leader of a new world. He clasped Francis's hand with both of his like he was grateful for the chance to know Francis again.

"You'll have to start training immediately."

"Anything." Said Francis.

"Your vessels will leave in three months time. Three men will train you. You must draw a map of the areas to be mined and of where the families are that will go with you. A draftsman will assist you."

"Yes sir." Said Francis.

Errlus reached for the intercom button. "Jason," he called. "Come in and escort Mr. Benevieve to his room."

"Thank you sir." Francis shook Errlus's hand again. "If my child's a boy, I'll name him after you. You're saving the lives of over 25 people on that mountain. Jason came in and they left.

Errlus stood for a few moments looking at the door. Then he walked to the wall that separated Andrea and himself. He depressed an indentation at the top and the scrim-like wall began to rise.

Andrea was sitting against the desk with her arms folded.

"How do you know: 'pregnant women miscarry'? Why do you care about a man who is unpredictable and irresponsible? Why not just turn him in for the reward? Considering what he did, it will be a substantial amount?"

"And what was that nonsense about your father saving the Earth to be as it is today? Are you mad as well as that nut you were just talking to?" Andrea swung around toward Errlus who had been listening quietly as she ranted on.

"There are many reasons that you do not have to know about now. I believe it is time for you to return to your cell." He looked at her half-eaten meal. "You've hardly eaten your lunch. I'll have another sent to you in your cell. I have to be alone now." He went to his desk and sat down, pushed the button on the blotter.

"Perkins, come in and escort Mrs. Anderson to her cell and be sure to have another lunch ready for her."

"Good day Mrs. Anderson."

Perkins entered and they left the room.

Errlus took out a letter from an envelope in his desk. He unfolded it and looked at the painting briefly while saying to himself, "Well father, there's so much I wish I could tell you." Then, he started to write. It was a letter that would travel back centuries. With a seal on it that would forbid its opening until Francis Benevieve's son's 18th birthday, the birthday after Errlus's own disappearance from his family in a time cell. That day his father would realize exactly who he had met in a room beside a man-made volcano beneath a future ocean on a planet only his oldest son would see again.

In the letter, Errlus instructed Francis of the precautions he would need to make and the provisions he would have to secure for the time 1623 years in the future of Ganymede when Francis's 17 year old son, Errlus—a namesake to himself—would arrive and need to be trained to save 375 families from a burning world. Much later their descendants would repopulate an Earth that spontaneously combusted just after the last of Francis's ships broke from its orbit. The purulent, vaporous world that Francis would soon be sent back in time to save would colonize Ganymede, a distant moon; so that Francis's pregnant wife could carry their unborn son to the new world where he would be born in a few months time only to disappear when he was 17 years old, reappear 1623 years later to be trained to become the time pirate his father now sought due to a passion for a woman born over a thousand years before his own birth, a woman who would bear him a daughter and three sons, the first of whom would be Errlus, the Time Pirate.

CHAPTER 16

THE LETTER

Francis was tired, but he stayed up till the first sunbeams entered his son's room. It would be his son's 18th birthday. Just a few hours earlier this 18th birthday, his son disappeared in one of the time cells used by the people of his new world. Mindolyn was with him. She folded her arms waiting. Francis carried the letter to his son's bed, sat on the neatly arranged blankets and opened up the letter given to him by Errlus. He had kept his promise not to open it until his son's 18th birthday. He wondered if Errlus could have known that his son would not be there on that day.

The room seemed so empty and cold. He felt like his son was dead to him. His first born, the reason he went to Errlus for help in rescuing Mindolyn from a past death was lost somewhere in time. He wasn't sure if he had gone to the "Past" or "Future". The other time machines no longer functioned. Once used, they never came back. Some chemical must have been missing. The time cell his son had taken was the last vessel. He opened the letter, read the 1st line and felt like a wave of liquid pulsed fresh life into his tired body.

The letter began:

> *"Dear Father: There is so much you must do. First,
> please know this fact: the man you spoke to long ago to
> save your future wife was actually the son she would
> later deliver. Now you must ready your scientists for
> my return. It is centuries to come in the year 3640 but
> more ships will be needed...."*

Francis looked at Mindolyn. He started to read the letter aloud. The room grew lighter. The sun never before seemed so beautiful. *Their* son was alive and well in a future time, in a cleaner world, on the planet they had vacated when it started to burn inself into a sterilization pattern that they did not then understand. Their son was alive and they had to prepare their new world for their 17-year-old's return home in a time over a thousand years away.

**Francis Reads Errlus's Letter
on What Would Have Been Francis's Son's 18th Birthday.
It Begins: "Dear Father..."**

Mindolyn sat next to Francis and held his cheeks as she gazed into his eyes. This savior of her family had actually saved Earth's future by falling in love with her. She felt blessed. She put her arm around him as they continued to read their son's letter.

PART III

JOHANNAH—
THE TIME PIRATE'S WIFE:
BACK TO THE
FIERY MOON

PART III

JOHANNAH—
THE TIME PIRATE'S WIFE:
BACK TO THE
FIERY MOON

CHAPTER 17

FIRE DANCE

Bernard was ecstatic. The performance was stunningly executed. A limber man dressed like a jester in a half-black-and-half-red-costume that simulated fire danced and leapt across the floor like flames across a forest. Sometimes the flame figure seemed to be cradle-ing imaginary infants, then bowing to a ghost-like image of a woman, then kissing her hand, next courting her with flute music as he circled an area where he had knelt. His pointed hat had three sections of which each was divided into bright red and black with bells on each tip. It made a beautiful tinkling sound as he leapt across the floor. His mask was black and covered only the eyes of his two-toned painted face. During the drum and cymbal duet of increasingly loud and quick notes, the dancer fell to his knees, and then implored the sky with open arms that came down with his fist pounding the ground in indignation that switched back and forth from prayer to anger and back again. Shrill piano music pounded out with harmony switched to discord and prompted the dancer to leap across the stage like a wind-blown flame. Less than a year ago, this dancer—Popla, Andrea's son—had attempted suicide. Bernard clapped seconds after the music stopped as Popla bowed to the imaginary sky and audience as if overcome with emotion.

Surely now, after such a beautiful exhibition of life's joys and trials, Popla wanted to live. Bernard shouted: "BRAVO!" "BRAVO!" He patted Popla on the back and then shook his hand to congratulate him on his accomplishment. Surely someone who could demonstrate the highs and lows in life with such acrobatic and musical skill would not throw it away. Popla looked down at Bernard's smiling face and frowning like a man intent on a mission, he asked for the code to the sealed NR3 chamber.

Bernard's smile dropped. He had promised Andrea he would watch over Popla. How could he let the chamber be opened to the person he most wanted to keep away from it? He, himself, had mandated that it be shut down till a candidate had completed the prerequisite appropriately. No one, yet, had come close to illustrating the music he had played for the audience of NR3 candidates.

Now his enthusiasm for art betrayed him by his expressing approval of Popla's work. Popla had completed the "pre-requisite" exquisitely and there was no denying his success. Bernard should have acted "unmoved" or disappointed. He tried to salvage a chance at denying Popla his right to use the NR3 by smiling and saying, "Excellent for the first attempt! But my boy, there's so much more you can do."

In answer to this, Popla looked over at his two friends. They both shrugged. One said, "I told you." Popla started for the door with the other two while yelling to Bernard, "I knew you would not give in, but I have friends who believe they know how to use the chamber. You lied to me Bernard. I know the work was more than passable."

Bernard's heart was racing. He had promised Andrea that he would watch over her son. He knew the difficulty of the task but somehow he slipped up by praising a masterpiece. He had to honor his promise. He grabbed his coat, told his assistant that he would be back in a day or two, and then followed the three partners in suicide.

They were going to the NR3 chamber. He knew a shortcut, flagged a nearby cab, and arrived—he thought—ahead of them;

but he soon found evidence contrary to that belief. A red and black feather was stuck in the door. Popla must have entered there and let the door close on his costume. Bernard opened the exterior door, walked down the hallway. Cobwebs hung from the ceiling, dust seemed to hang in the air. The lights were dim. The Nothingness Room, the third of its kind in existence, had not been used since Bernard's performance of the music he had written as a tribute to his late sister. The music embodied all he ever felt in his life, the problem of being ostracized due to a disease that caused tumors to protrude from his skin, the love he had for his wife, the loss he felt when he realized she married him for publicity reasons, the passion he felt for talent or for the beauty of a storm, the love for his sister, the anguish he felt when she left him utterly alone, the surprise of being accepted into the art world of his time as a master playwright and musician, the pain once caused by a disease now cured.

Just before he had closed the NR3, his symphony had stirred the young people in the audience to applause. He remembered being in that drafty auditorium filled with people who wanted to commit suicide and he still got chills at the irony of applause from people who wished to be dead. He remembered telling them that the NR3 chamber would be closed to anyone who could not artistically come close to the meaning of the music he had played. Fortunately, no one had yet succeeded at the old fashioned kind of suicide and no one had yet come close to exhibiting the meaning of his music artistically until this morning when Popla performed with the help of his two friends.

Two sets of footprints lay in the dust. One of Popla's group must have taken a different route.

Bernard was at least 75 feet from the chamber. He ran to the end of the first hallway and just as he turned toward the hallway where the chamber was located, lights blinked for a few seconds and a huge humming sound whirled into a buzz. He arrived at the closed chamber door. Was he too late he wondered? The building smelt like burnt flesh and smoldering circuits. He pushed his way in. The room was empty. It smelt of chemicals, burnt dust, old meat and cologne. He tried to catch his breath but no air seemed to come. He reeled dizzily toward the door, and then fell weakly to the floor. Just before he passed out, a panel slid from the wall and there stood two men in gas masks who seemed to be holding a black and red feathered body.

"Popla...?!" he cried out incredulously. Then Bernard succumbed to blackness and dreams.

The men in gas masks were back to their old jobs, a job as old as the first Nothingness Room. Errlus needed recruits: why waste a life? Johannah, Errlus's wife had suggested rescuing young people from themselves by taking those who had signed up for the Nothingness Rooms from the first person ever to push the button inside one of those chambers to the last three who attempted to die after Johannah herself had died when a wall of lava hit her on the fiery moon called IO. By the time Popla and Bernard entered the chamber, all suicide candidates that pushed that button activated only a simulation of death by electricity. The first 110 had actually died and their deaths had to be stopped by arriving a few seconds before the button was pressed. After the first 110, the syndicate was in place enough to change the wiring of the rooms. The last three to use the NR3 before Popla activated it with his friends' help were: Sally Fitzgerald, Ahmed Smith, and Anthony Zelinski. Their reasons were similar to many of the candidates who chose death over existence. Most of the time it was joblessness. Sometimes it was just loneliness or a sense of being tricked out of receiving credit for hard work and skilled devotion. Sometimes it was all of this.

Sally Fitzgerald loved music. She had excelled in voice classes, piano lessons, flute, violin, and viola. She could even play the drums in a marching band as well as for an orchestra. Her passion was to write a symphony. She wanted to write music for 15 instruments in an arrangement that would last two hours.

In her junior year of college, her music theory teacher presented them with a project choice: either write two songs with vocals and 5 instruments each or write music for an hour-long symphony for

20 instruments. It was something Sally had already started. She had five weeks before it was due. She spent every waking hour of her weekends and all spare hours of her week nights writing, doing sound checks with a simulated instrument program, humming ideas then scribbling them down. Her friends gave up calling her. Her mother just tried to make sure she had enough to eat by placing sandwiches in front of her computer. Her brothers knew not to go near her room. Finally, it was done. It was written on the huge sheets of music paper her teacher had supplied. She had twenty-one copies to hand in as requested. The teacher distributed the class's work to band members for all the assignments. Each one was played during a week-long series of concerts except for Sally's.

The teacher instructed Sally to meet her in the classroom after school on Monday to discuss her work. She handed back 20 copies to Sally saying. "Remember, I told you that plagiarism would not get you a better grade. You have till the end of the week to complete the assignment or you'll be close to failing.

Sally was devastated. It *was* an original work. *How could her teacher say it wasn't?* She tried to point out that she had not copied it at all. The teacher would not listen.

Sally wrote two 5-piece songs and handed it in at the end of the week. The teacher gave her 75 out of 100 for a grade.

The next year was graduation. She graduated with honors but felt like every lesson was a drudgery to accomplish. She felt like all her efforts would somehow be thwarted. Every effort seemed exhausting. A year after graduating, she still could not find a job in music anywhere. Even the waitress jobs were difficult to acquire. Then she heard her symphony on the radio. It was the first time she had heard it played. The announcer raved about the piece and said that a woman who used to work as a teacher wrote it. It was Sally's teacher. Sally was devastated. Her confidante, her mentor had stolen her work and there was nothing she could do about it. To make matters worse, her father and mother disappeared on a skiing trip. All their money was left to her and her brothers but the void Sally felt was so intense that the few times she would visit her brothers was not enough. They were busy with college and work. She signed up for the NR3 without them knowing.

Sally went into the large empty room, saw the metallic grey walls, and watched as the attendant placed a box with a red button attached to an extension cord that went outside the room. She looked around, went to the box after the chamber was secured, stepped on the button. The room seemed to spin, there was a zapping noise, and then she was gone. The next person walked in a half-hour later. His name was Ahmed. He had studied to be an architect. No firms were hiring. All jobs were filled with well-known architects desperate for new work. Jobs were scarce. In that day where most people lived to be 200 years old on average, many people kept their jobs for over a hundred years. A work week normally consisted of only 20 hours of work per week but still, there were so many skilled people that new jobs rarely opened up to a college grad. Young people were living off their parents. Most parents did not mind. Money was not a problem but they looked at their own children with pity, as if the problem was in their child—not in society. Ahmed's parents would roll their eyes a lot when he told them about the scarcity of interviews available. They thought he did not try enough. They let him stay in their beach house in the summer and their mountain villa in the fall; but he felt useless. They laughed at his idea to build a small round cabin in the woods. They poured two shot glasses of scotch and chugged them down quick and poured another as he told them about his idea to build a 100-foot high light house near their summer home. They had the money but thought the ideas too silly to support. They smiled and said not to worry about working. Ahmed's parent's asked a friend to hire him for a few months. Ahmed learned the office was well-staffed with 20-hour a week working relatives of rich architects. Most of these "connected" co-workers hated their jobs but just wanted to keep their parents happy. His ideas became their ideas. Then, after a few months, he was let go. His parents were visiting a Greek isle. He signed up for the NR3.

Anthony, the very last person to use the NR3 before Bernard shut it down, was different. He loved his family, enjoyed school, had two very special friends, and reveled in fashion and interior design. He had designed the clothes for high-school musicals and helped design clothes for college shows and eventually was designing costumes for the best musicals in the hemisphere where he lived; but then his parents disappeared on a cruise ship and his best friends were busy in their own lives. Everyone he knew was a business acquaintance and he felt empty. The work load decreased and his days were filled with meals and sleep but nothing else. He signed up for the NR3. Fashion was losing it's fascination for him. There was no one to share it with.

Like Popla, these three went into the metallic-walled chamber and pressed the button left for the suicidal. They felt the dizzy sensation of gases they thought came from smoldering circuits for a brief few seconds. Electricity zapped across the room and panels slid away as men in gas masks lifted their new recruits into a gurney and transported them to a cell in Errlus's syndicate of "thieves". Errlus had colonies to fill with "volunteers". Some of the best "volunteers" would be in environments that were life-threatening. The best people for the job would need to not fear death. Errlus needed the NR3 to supply early Ganymede with people to mine the man-made caves constructed to hold a gravitational control system that would create a better atmosphere eventually on Jupiter's Earth-like moon.

Sally would be sent to Ganymede in the year 3655 to help young people enjoy life through music. Ahmed would be sent to Ganymede's oldest recorded day to assist with creating homes for Ganymede's early years when the atmosphere was devoid of oxygen and homes had to have their own supply of plant-life and shipments of oxygen or water to create hydrogen and oxygen. Anthony would need to be handled carefully. A team was set up to study each NR3 participant's life to find their goals and loves. Anthony basically chose to die out of loneliness. When it was discovered that Anthony's parents had been recruited from a cruise ship mission, the team assigned to his case located the parents and had them waiting for him when he woke out of his drugged sleep. He would have to be trained to maintain friendships outside of work so that life would be interesting to him. Anthony would go on in a future time to decorate homes with flowers known to produce large amounts of oxygen. He would also use these flowers as inspiration for floral designs that were used for centuries on both Earth and Ganymede.

Eventually Sally re-wrote her musical. It was a hit on Ganymede and eventually was performed on Earth before she was born there. She used her married name with her middle name to copyright the work. Marietta Quinn's musical was performed in Opera houses after "Sally" (Marietta Quinn) wrote the vocal parts. Later, when Sally Fitzgerald's teacher would accuse her of plagiarizing a work in order for that teacher to claim the work as her own, that teacher would be accused of plagiarism. This would occur three years after Sally went into the NR3 chamber. The team Errlus assigned to assist Sally made sure that a letter and newspaper article from Earth's future reached "Sally" (Marietta Quinn) to explain what happened to the teacher who stole her symphony. "Sally" was pleased to find out her musical was such a success. She felt vindicated somewhat that her former teacher had been accused of plagiarism. She pitied her somewhat because she understood the desire to achieve. She had forgiven her long ago and remembered the good things this teacher had taught her about music. She wished her well but wished her to be wiser and kinder in the future. This teacher was banned from ever teaching music again. She opened up a nursery school and eventually had three children of her own. She taught them not to steal and to enjoy all kinds of music.

The monitoring of the lives of people who subjected themselves to the NR3's function proved to be a valuable way to maintain life in all the colonies: early Ganymede, Earth (when it was safe to return, 2000 years after the spontaneous combustion of all landfills occurred), on the moon called IO during the creation of mining camps, and also in times when culture seemed so stagnant that suicide rates would increase. Johannah had figured that five people working together as a team for each NR3 candidate could find the trigger that would make a person want to live. Her suggestion became a standard procedure and it created jobs. Errlus relied on her ability to empathize with practically anyone to secure the stability of the leaders he chose for the numerous tasks involved in creating gravity, atmosphere, and plant-life on stagnant moons and on Earth after the toxic fires died out. Errlus needed the NR3 to be functional. When Popla and Bernard walked into that chamber, Errlus's men knew the NR3 would be running again soon. Errlus would be pleased.

CHAPTER 18

JOHANNAH SCHOOLS

Andrea was enraged. She was actually just dismissed from Errlus's presence as if she were a castaway toy. He had treated her like a confidante and then, when she asked relevant questions, he seemed disinterested in talking any further and had her sent back to finish her lunch in her 10 by 12 foot room. The only things in her cell were a cot, a toilet and sink, a tray with her now discarded lunch, a desk with an antiqued bible, and a new chair which had been brought in to replace the one she had broken into splinters. Unfortunately, they had swept the cell clean and the two-inch piece of metal she had taken from the first broken chair was gone. She checked the new chair to see if it also had that thin piece of metal. She took off the cushion, pulled at the backing, found the thin metal that locked the wooden pieces in place.

Later she would break the leg to get the piece to pop out. She was thinking that she may be able to use it to pick the lock of her cell. She would have to disguise her intent by throwing a tantrum as if she were stir-crazy from being imprisoned too long. All she could do for now was read that bible. It was printed in the year 14 in a place she had never heard about. It began: "In the beginning, there was Errlus, and he supplied all."

How contrived it was! She felt like screaming at the audacity of such of blatant piece of propaganda. Why was Errlus making himself out to be a god of some kind.

She skipped to page 153 and read, "The seventh ship arrived in the new world with 30 people. Unlike the rest, they came from three different mountains. It was getting more difficult to find survivors…"

Some of the pages were so brittle, they broke into pieces.

Andrea opened the book to the middle. There she read about schools being set up. They were called "Johannah schools". Why, she wondered. After Errlus's wife?

According to the book, Errlus had not arrived yet in their world as a young man but schools were being set up to model young women after his wife—before he even married. He was to have his pick. For over a thousand years, young girls born to most families on Ganymede had the first name of "Johannah". They all wanted to be Errlus's wife. This type of preparation was going on for centuries. Other preparations for the time cell arrival that would deliver a 17-year-old Errlus were also repeated for centuries. No one knew when he would arrive. She flipped a few pages forward, read a little more of what seemed "hero worship" or "a glorified, sanctimonious autobiography by Errlus".

She stood up in the sealed, four-walled cell. It was time. She stretched her arms to the ceiling wondering where the cameras were and hoping to disguise her actions. She punched the desk, kicked the chair, pulled the cushion to tear the material from its backing. She threw the chair against the wall, then went over to the broken leg and pulled loose the chair part she needed. Then she took another larger chair part and swung it around her head and smashed it against the wall. It cracked; she picked it up and swung again mumbling, "Johannah schools, humpff!" The chair dented the plaster and broke into pieces.

CHAPTER 19

PUMPKIN PIE

Something fell. His wife apologized as she bent to pick up wooden trays from the floor.

How could it be? His wife was there, making pies. She never made pies. But there she was looking picture perfect in a room that seemed to glow from all the windows. She smiled radiantly, bending toward him with a tray and a sample piece of cherry pie. It filled his nostrils and her hair had a perfume that smelled like pumpkin. Odd scents he thought: cherry pie and pumpkin. Then something tugged at his arm and a strange deep voice said, "These recruits must have gotten an extra dose."

Did his wife say that; he wondered as the glowing windows became lights that glared at him from above? Beside him was someone trying to position a tray of food.

"Yeah, they slept through breakfast—brought in last night. Try shaking him again."

Bernard was ravenous. The pie smelled great. There were two trays. One was beside his bunk… the other was beside another bunk. He couldn't see quite well yet.

"Where am I?" he stammered.

"Ah, you're awake. Good. Eat. You have been asleep longer than usual. Ask questions later old man. We are your friends." The deep voiced young man handed him a tray.

He saw the cherry pie. Where was the pumpkin? He looked around at the blurry room.

"Thank you." Bernard said. He was grateful, curious and concerned all at once but mostly he was hungry.

On the tray, there was soup, bean soup with parsley sprigs. There was bread and cheese, mustard, lettuce, tomato slices, black and green olives in a bowl, hot stuffing with gravy and potatoes, moist turkey, milk and cherry pie with what looked like homemade crust. He took a bite of the cherry pie first and heard a moan. He blinked to clear his eyes to look more carefully at what he was eating.

Over by the other tray was a blanket covering someone. Red and black feathers stuck out from the top of the bunk. Odd colors to wear he thought, then, he remembered Popla. Popla had used the NR3— gone. But there he was. He remembered seeing the moving panels, seeing Popla's lifeless body and those men with masks, gas masks. That smell which made his head spin. The darkness enveloped him then until—his wife dropped that stack of trays while making pies. And now here he was and Popla was alive. He took another bite of cherry pie. It tasted better than any he had ever had. He still smelled a pumpkin flavor. He looked over at the blanketed feathered person he figured was Popla.

"Popla! It looks like we've been shanghaied but—good news.— you're alive enough to enjoy that pumpkin pie you have."

"Shanghaied—What!?" Popla said struggling to open his eyes. He was surprised that death still allowed him senses. He was hungry and he thought he could smell pumpkin pie and stuffing with turkey gravy. He remembered going to the NR3 chamber, pushing the button, seeing the bright lights, feeling the heat, smelling the burnt circuits and the smell of burnt hair, then he saw a blackness as two dark black holes were crushing him then pulling him apart. Then there was this dream of Olivia and pies and Bernard's voice saying something about philosophy. He opened his eyes and saw rectangular lights blaring down on him. He must still be alive. He lifted his arm and saw the red and black sleeve of the costume he wore for Bernard's "prerequisite". For a second, he wondered if he was in the afterlife and dealing with some type of punishment: hunger, the smell of food, and Bernard were his punishments. He sat up to look around. Yes, Bernard was there. He must be in Hell he thought.

Then he saw the tray with gravy and slices of meat, stuffing with celery and was it, onions, and to the side... pumpkin pie.

Bernard said, "Enjoy Popla. If it's an afterlife dream, it tastes real."

Popla took a fork from the tray and reached over to scoop some stuffing then dip it in the steaming gravy. He put it in his mouth. He never remembered it ever tasting so good, so fulfilling. His mouth practically tingled with the sense of taste.

"Wow, Bernard, what a flavor."

"Yes, better than I expected." said Bernard. "It looks like we are still alive and captives in this 10 x 12 foot room... and our captors have excellent cooks."

"But the chamber—I pushed the button—and everything got hot, and dark."

Bernard took another bite of his cherry pie, and then laughed as if realizing the implications and the main purpose of those Nothingness Rooms.

Popla continued: "I was in a park with Olivia. She was swinging on an old swing. Then, what... what happened... I should be gone."

Bernard laughed, happy that Andrea's son was still alive.

"How do you know if this isn't what happens after death, waking up in a room while ravenously hungry and offered food."

"Stop joking." Popla said.

"Well, it's better than being ravenously hungry and not having food." added Bernard.

Popla smelled the pumpkin pie and had to agree.

"True." He said. He looked at the pie. Beside it was the bowl of stuffing. He picked it up to smell it closer. His mouth watered. He took another mouthful.

"Wow." He said. "It's amazing."

Bernard had to agree. He rambled on:

"I think it's partly an effect of whatever drug they used to knock us out: a person wakes up hungry. Of course, we could have been out for days for all I know; that'll make a person hungry. They sure have a good cook. The meat is so tender, cooked just right. Coffee. Haven't had coffee like this in ages."

Popla chimed in, "Man, I've never been this hungry." Popla took another bite of stuffing. "It just melts." He grabbed a fork of meat, put it in his mouth, and just held it there. He was glad to be alive enough to taste it; but angry that his goal to die had been robbed from him. The conflict caused some self-loathing—but the food—was too amazing to stop. He held each bite of his food in his mouth for a few seconds without chewing, closed his eyes and tried to remember where he had tasted it before. He thought, "Weekend dinners".

"Ah—that's..." Popla bent his head toward the floor as it seemed heavy with memories. Tears formed in the corners of his eyes.

"Man… the memories…. I forgot those times." He shook his head. "She was so happy then."

Bernard was glad to see these emotions in Popla.

"Who?" he asked.

Popla looked at Bernard, almost grateful for the company. "My mother. I remember her with her apron on, putting plates on the table. The food was so good. I was eleven then, I think. She rarely cooked. Dad seemed surprised at the taste of everything. Later, we found delivery boxes in the kitchen from a local restaurant. She had pretended that she had cooked all day but actually had been working on a paper for a speech she was writing. Man, that food was so good… like this."

"Good to be alive sometimes." Bernard stated.

Popla looked at him, smiled, took another bite and nodded as he shut his eyes remembering.

Bernard thought to himself how odd it was that extreme hunger, followed immediately by well-cooked food could possibly cure the suicidal. He took a long sip of slightly hot coffee that tasted better than any he had ever tasted. He wondered why these people abducted him and Popla. Was it just because Popla was the son of a continent leader? Was it because they wanted Bernard himself for some reason? Had they done this abduction thing before? Were they "shanghaied" (an old term he remembered from his early English classes) for some foreign legion? Who ran things? He figured his captors would fill him in later. Till then, he would just enjoy the food before him. The crust was flaky with just the right amount of butter. The cherries were immersed in a slightly sweet glaze. The salad had bread crumbs, toasted and seasoned with rosemary. The drumstick was crusty and moist at the same time. Popla was safe from attempting suicide for a few days at least. Andrea's trust was still honored. Popla, her remorseful son, was still alive.

CHAPTER 20

LAVA CREATURE

Fiery Figure Stands Before Errlus's Son

The wall of lava was moving towards his son and wife who stood just 20 feet away, then Jason pulled him into the time cell and sealed the door. But just before the door slid shut, he saw a feathery, fiery, black and red figure grab his son who seemed transfixed by the figure. Was it a figment of his imagination? Did a foreign people live on that faraway moon? Who wears something like that on a rescue mission? He figured his eyes had been playing tricks on him and never mentioned it to anyone. Errlus had fallen asleep after writing the letter to his father. The dream was a recurring one. Sometimes he would see his son disappear. Sometimes he would see his wife hit by a stone that knocked her out. Once he saw her encapsulated in a diamond coffin after she fell. The coffin grew around her as if it rose out of the ground, then a crystal door slid over her just before the lava hit and it sank back in the ground. Was it a dream? Or had he actually seen it just before Jason pulled him into the timecell? The coffin looked as if it had been carved out of a diamond or put together by diamond blocks. Diamond blocks. Could a diamond cylinder save a person from a wall of lava?

Someone was knocking on the door. It had been a short sleep. Jason came into the office and mentioned that the NR3 was briefly back in service and it had brought them two new recruits rather than one. Errlus thanked Jason who he had noticed had a slight smirk on his face. He looked at him curiously.

"You'll never believe what one of them was wearing: Red and black tights with black feathers."

**Fiery Figure Wearing Red and Black Feathers
Stands Before Errlus's Son**

Errlus knew exactly who had been brought in by the NR3 crew. It was Andrea's son, a catalyst to getting Andrea to sign on with his network; but this was new. Was Andrea's son the person he saw trying to rescue his own son from a wall of lava? This reinforced his conviction to go ahead with the mission. Bernard was an added bonus because without him, more candidates would eventually find their way to the chamber to attempt suicide, then he would have more recruits for the difficult tasks involved in creating an atmosphere on a dead planet. Suicidal people did not fear much and were expendable. But the costume Jason described was a sketchy piece of his memory that he could not forget.

"Jason, is the fellow so thin that he looks like he's made out of twigs?"

Jason looked surprised, "Yes sir. But how did you know."

"Is it Bernard... or Andrea's son?"

"The older man calls the guy, 'Popla'".

"Has Andrea picked the lock to her cell yet?" Errlus asked.

"Not that I know of sir."

"Make sure all other doors but the one to "Popla's" cell are sealed. Watch that corridor. An hour after she gets into Bernard and Popla's cell, bring all three to see me.

"Yes sir." Jason said while trying not to seem surprised at Errlus knowing the captives names. "Will do."

Errlus felt almost grateful that the pieces were finally coming together. He knew this Popla fellow would do anything for the woman he loved and he knew that Olivia was the woman who Popla had loved enough to marry but she turned him down to "travel". He knew now that Olivia must miss feeling loved. So a once suicidal man may just be the best volunteer he could get to save his son; but he still needed someone to rescue Johannah. It had something to do with that diamond coffin... or was it a cylinder.

He sat down at his desk to try to sketch the placement of the fiery figure, his son, his fallen wife, and the diamond wall around her. It appeared that the black and red feathery figure he thought he had seen may have actually been more memory then illusion. If everything continued to go well, the things he had planned would occur: Andrea would sign on in return for her son having Olivia back; Olivia would go to Popla because Popla unconditionally loved her and Errlus had made sure that his treatment of her made her feel "unloved"; and Popla would volunteer to rescue Errlus's own son for Olivia. Who could he get to save Johannah? He could not save her himself because he died once trying. Jason was too valuable.

They could not go back to the time before the eruptions occurred because of the gold deposits discovered and because, the moment after the first eruption, he saw his wife slap the face of the man he had thought was her lover. She had slapped him and then pulled a knife on the man and told him to leave. Then she called Errlus on a cell phone and complained about the insubordination of the man. Errlus had been going crazy with jealousy but when she turned to him first, all the months of suspicion had gone away. Then the quakes started and he had to rush to get to Johannah's side. The mining for the gold discovery had started a chain reaction.

Gold was needed for more time cells. Johannah was needed for his peace of mind and his son's life was worth more than gold to him. Now he knew how to save all concerned. He would have to wait for the people he needed to fall into the patterns he set and soon he would be able to go ahead to the next five-year check point with his wife and son and enough gold to keep all the settlements functioning. He had to figure how to create a cylinder made of the hardest substance known to man, place time cells in strategic places and then rescue the people he loved most. He knew all this could be done. All he needed was time. And time was easy to control for an errorless man. His mother had told him that he was named after such a person, the benefactor who gave their people ships to leave a fiery world for a new chance at life. She did not know that that benefactor was actually her son, an errorless man named after himself who needed the gentle strength of a well-raised woman to continue the missions that saved thousands of generations of different civilizations. He had read the bible that told him all this before, but he never believed it to be totally true till hearing of the costume that Popla wore to the NR3 chamber. Destiny was a bible he never wrote nor believed in but his faith was returning and soon his wife would be returned as well.

CHAPTER 21

HERO OR HEROINE

There was a knock on the cell room door. Jason figured he would announce his entrance before attempting to enter a cell that now held three prisoners, one of whom was overzealous.

"Hello Mr. Hopkins, Popla, Mrs. Anderson. Please be aware, we know you are all together. Glad you had a chance to greet each other.

"Please be aware, I have a team of soldiers with me and Errlus requests a meeting with all of you together. As I open the door, please come out calmly."

Andrea was irritated. Their cells must all be monitored visually. Perhaps they even planted the pin that let her unlock her cell for some reason.

At least she had gotten to speak with Popla. He looked utterly ridiculous in that costume but apparently, according to Bernard, he was gifted at choreography. She had always thought dancing to be a silly career. Deep down she hoped he would fall in love with some type of vocation. She was tickled about hearing about the flute, alarmed about the poetry and devastated about his damaged wrists. He had been through so much.

They walked along the corridors more curious than concerned. The rounded edges appeared to be put together like a ship more than a building.

The meeting room they were brought into was huge. Errlus had green tea, water and a fruit tray with cheese and rolls ready for them. As soon as Popla walked in, he went to him and shook his hand vigorously. The costume he wore was just like the one he had seen before Jason had grabbed him to keep him from trying to rescue his son a second time. The first time, it had ended in failure but then immediately afterward a feathery creature stood between his son and the wall of lava. He remembered seeing the tall, lanky creature leap in two jumps toward his son, grab him, then jump onto a rock somehow perched above the steamy hot river of debris. He wasn't sure but he seemed to remember the rock formation that the lanky figure jumped toward looked like a submarine. This would make sense. The strangest thing about the feathery creature was that it appeared to be wearing a costume. Popla was wearing the same exact costume.

After shaking Popla's hand, he offered his "prisoners" some refreshments.

Andrea was stunned. Errlus was treating her son as if he had been an operative of some sort. Either Errlus was greatly mistaken or her son had been living a double life.

Bernard felt a bit left out but he was used to feeling like a fly on the wall. He figured sometimes such a seat had the best views.

Andrea sat down on the chairs provided as did Bernard but Popla was asked to stand on a slightly raised 4 foot by 12 foot platform against the wall. Errlus insisted he stand on a white "X" positioned toward the right of the platform.

He instructed Jason to dim the lights and start the video.

The wall lit up with fire and smoke. Volcanoes behind where Popla stood looked so dangerously close that Andrea almost jumped toward Popla to pull him away. Popla's back was to them but just in back of Popla was a costumed image that looked just like him. He turned to look at what Bernard and Andrea were horrified to see. It was beautiful and horrifying at the same time. Errlus had Jason stop the video, then asked Popla to stand beside the costumed figure.

"Ah, just as I thought." Said Errlus. "You were *not* the figure I saw back on that firey moon. But, you may be able to tell me who exactly has a costume just like the one you are wearing."

Popla looked intently at the image. "Can you make it larger?" he asked.

The image of a red haired, black masked, stick figure covered half the wall. It was almost skeletal.

"I believe this person is the maker of the costume. Billy Joe. I can't believe she would attempt something like this though. She's not well, very sickly lately. She helped me with my costume between heading to chemo treatments. She was always skipping them though because they made her feel worse and she felt there was just too much to do."

"Can you give me her full name?" Errlus asked directly.

"Billy Joe Wringley. She lives not far from where Bernard's Art Center is. She used to go there everyday till the walk seemed like too much."

Jason looked at Errlus as if he read his mind. "I'll get someone right on it sir." He left the room.

Andrea was the first to ask, "What is this person to you Errlus?" she asked congenially.

Errlus smiled. "This person may have saved my son... or actually, may be the only one who is able to save him since he has not yet been rescued. Just before Jason pulled me into the timecell that saved my life, I saw this image. We sent video cameras back to the time to analyze where I was when the timecell landed, where my son stood, whether the fiery figure was real and where my wife was exactly before the wall of lava hit us—them." Errlus stared intently at the picture.

"See that glint of white to the far right. I cannot figure what it is."

Bernard walked up to the wall and looked at it closely. "Can you make that area larger?" he asked.

Errlus went to a remote control and enlarged the area. Bernard looked at it intently. "Leggos. It looks like leggos. Who would make a wall of leggos out of—" he looked closer and seemed surprised—"diamonds?"

Errlus looked intently at Bernard. "What are leggos?" he asked.

Bernard looked perplexed for a moment with the thought that he had actually outlived Leggos.

"Leggos are a children's toy. They're actually building blocks that fit together. Normally they are only an inch in size but these look like they're the size of cinder blocks."

Errlus asked, "Do you know where I can find these blocks?"

Bernard said, "No, but I believe I know who can find the information you need." He was thinking of Gwendolyn. She knew research parameters extremely well. "Gwendolyn Doucet Montgomery". Andrea looked curiously at Bernard. What was he up to she wondered.

Errlus talked to the intercomm, "Anthony, locate Gwendolyn Doucet Montgomery, Jonas' daughter and bring her to this facility."

"She's with child. Could you warn your men to be careful due to her condition." Bernard cautioned.

Errlus smiled. "Don't worry Bernard. They are always careful." Just as he said this, a sound like a stack of dishes falling was heard over the intercomm. Errlus looked at Bernard's concerned expression. And added, "And Anthony…." He waited for a reply.

"Yes, Errlus."

"Make note that Mrs. Montgomery is with child and should be treated with extreme gentleness, consideration, and respect."

"Will do, Sir. Oh and by the way sir, that noise… we got it sir, just some dishes."

"Things happen. Be more cautious next time." Errlus said while looking at Bernard's still worried expression.

Then he looked at Andrea and said, "So, are you ready to join our team yet Mrs. Anderson?"

"You think because you compliment my son and insist upon the care of a person you are about to abduct that I'm ready to sign on to your crew of thieves?"

"Not yet, I take it, but you should know, if it wasn't for my network of "thieves", society would have ended back in 3057 when the world spontaneously combusted. You, Mrs. Anderson, if your line of family survived, would be living like cave people without those of us who use time travel to assist. When things calmed down on Earth, we brought people back from our settlements to repopulate. I didn't plan this. The people trained by my father prepared me for sending back the missions and setting up the encampments and he started this training after I left his encampment in a time cell when I was 17." He looked at Popla who looked just a little older than 17. He figured maybe he would understand what he was about to say.

"A friend of mine and I went into the time cell that had been momentarily unguarded. Unbeknownst to me he pushed some buttons just before he ran out. The door started to close. I figured it would open in a minute. I looked at all the lights blinking, the thing started to spin. I actually fell into the seat. I was surprised how quickly it could move. It had been idle for years. I was pressed into the seat. I remember gripping the armrests and wondering if it was defective. Then, it slowed down and stopped. It was only fifteen minutes. The door was being opened from the outside. I figured it was my friend Steve, the one who pushed the buttons. A bunch of people in lab coats were there with clip boards. There must have been 25 people standing there and the room was no longer a shack with a guard but a 300 square-foot lab with 20 foot high ceilings and lights as bright as the sun." He looked at Popla who was listening intently. "...And just beyond the men and women with clipboards, stood a girl who I thought was my age. Her lab coat was a rose color.

She was only 18 but close up, she looked 12. She actually already had a phD in physics. She was there with her cousin. Apparently it was her turn to be in the lab at that time. All the people in white lab coats were clapping and talking amongst themselves and I just felt drawn to that rose-colored lab coat. She just stood there with her arms behind her back. I went over to her and asked, "What's all the fuss about?" She looked at me quizically saying, "You don't know." In a surprised voice. Then she looked into my eyes as if she saw my soul and took my hand saying, "Well, I have a lot to tell you." The year was 3640 on that particular moon. The year I left was 2017. In 15 minutes, I had travelled 1,623 years. That woman in the pink lab coat… later became my wife and you Popla, you may be able to help me get her back."

Popla felt honored but was wary. This was the man who Olivia had left to go follow.…. This was the man who wrecked his life just by being alive and here he was treating him like a comrade in arms. Popla didn't speak and he tried not to glare at him with the anger smoldering beneath his placid exterior. Somehow the anger was diminishing and gradually being replaced with a strange sense of honor and pride.

"Open your eyes Mrs. Anderson. Once my wife is back, I'll need someone like you to be an ally, not a prisoner because once everything is secured here, then I must travel five more years ahead to maintain the settlements in the past and the newer settlements in the ever-changing present. Someone like you will be needed to make sure men like Jonas don't get to take on too much of a vigilante role."

Andrea felt annoyed. He was talking down to her. "It appears, Errlus, that men like Jonas are a major reason for your existence." She was referring to Jonas' mission that sent men back to the year 3054 in Earth's time where one of the men disobeyed orders and fathered a son with a chieftain's daughter.

"You're coming around Mrs. Anderson."

"How dare he be so familiar and pedantic!" thought Andrea as she was being led back to her cell. She started wondering: "What

CATHERINE MARIE WEISS-CELLEY

if Errlus were right?" A chill ran through her right down to her bones and she pushed the thought out of her head and figured she could discuss things with Gwendolyn soon. She looked at Popla. Somehow he seemed to look wiser. For some reason he appeared to have a newfound sense of nobility she thought. Amazing what a compliment can do.

CHAPTER 22

BILLY JOE AND GWEN

The women for the job were before him. One was the tall, lanky stringbean of a woman who designed the fire-red costume worn by a supposed rescuer of Errlus' son, Atticus. The other was a very pregnant research specialist intercepted on her way to the Darii lands. Errlus greeted them both by shaking their hands. Behind him was the volcanic scene with the costumed figure standing just before his son. Billy Joe was staring at the wall but had not yet seen the costumed figure on the right.

"Is this a painting or a photograph?"

Then she saw the right –hand corner where the costume she designed appeared to be worn by someone who looked like her.

"Do you see the boy before your image?"

"My image?" she said incredulously while amazed that anyone could even stand in such a place.

"Why would I ever have volunteered for a job like that? Is that a backdrop? It looks so real."

Billy Joe Wrigley was a costume designer, set designer, playwright and actress. She had been fighting cancer for years and had not yet been cured partly because the medicine interfered with her work and she did not believe she could be cured at this point.

"It's not a backdrop. It's one of the moons of Jupiter and I believe that person you see there is you. You're standing before my son. Watch this." Errlus pushes a button on the wall and the image becomes a movie scene as the costumed figure leaps to grab the 12-year-old boy, then jumps to a rock that looks like a submarine.

"I have reason to believe that this is your future." Errlus said.

Billy Joe was overwhelmed. She sat in one of the chairs provided as if she couldn't stand much longer.

"I can't even lift a sack of potatoes but a 12-year old boy." She shook her head in disbelief.

"Well, I have a team of doctors and physical trainers that will work with you day and night. What you have is an acute leukemia but it is curable. With the diet designed for your needs, the exercise routines, the medicine, you should be ready for stunts like this in six-months time. Are you willing to help me get my son back."

Billy Joe ran her fingers through her hair. She had heard of Errlus before through the grapevines in the theatre world. She was an admirer of his drive. She stood up and walked over to shake his hand.

"It would be an honor." She said.

"Good. Your room is ready. Jason will escort you. He is just outside. Rest a while, a trainer will wake you and escort you to a work-out session."

"Thank you Errlus."

"You are most welcome. Thank you for helping me save my son." Billy Joe left the room.

"Now, Ms. Doucet or do you prefer Mrs. Montgomery."

Gwendolyn was feeling the uncomfortable stages of pregnancy. She did not care. "Just call me Gwen. Now, you don't expect me to leap-frog through fire to save anyone do you?"

"No." He laughed. "But a friend of yours has told me you are an expert at research. And I need to know how to make Leggos."

What a word. "Leggos?" said Gwendolyn.

Errlus seemed dismayed that she did not already know what they were. "Bernard said you would be able to get designs of these toy blocks."

"Bernard—" Now Gwendolyn had to sit down.

"Are you okay, Gwen?" Errlus was concerned that she may be close to her due date.

"Yes. Sometimes my feet feel like butter."

"Yes. Some things or people do that to a person. I take it you know Bernard very well then." Errlus asked politely.

"Bernard may just be this baby's father. There's a chance, though... that the baby's father is a man... who raped me. This "rapist" had been a very reputable man at one time but... he was in a drugged, feverous state. I am hoping the child is Bernard's."

Now Errlus felt a need to sit down, but he remained standing. He knew that it was Gwen who helped Francis after Francis arrived from the past mission that eventually saved his mother and himself from dying in that ancient time. If Gwendolyn were pregnant from Francis, the baby inside of her could be his brother or sister and his father could be branded a rapist.

"Are *you* alright Errlus?" She was surprised at his sudden lack of concentration.

"Yes." He sat down. "I am so sorry for your having to deal with such—with a possible rape. Did you think of prosecuting the culprit?"

"He was a man desperate to save someone he loved. He confused me with her. His friend had drugged him to bring him back to this time. When he spoke of this "Mindolyn" I wished it was my husband saying that name. I almost gave in. I bit him to bring him out of his... delirium; but there's a chance I did not stop him in time."

"Your husband, ah, yes. He died in that horrific fire some years ago."

"And my father refused to go back in time to stop him from entering that car with my son. I can never forgive him for that."

"Gwen." Errlus said. "I can send someone back to rescue them, but, they will not be able to stay in that location."

Errlus said what she had been longing to hear. "Errlus, if you can save them somehow, I will do my best to find the information you need."

"We have a deal then."

"Deal." They shook hands. Then Errlus told her she would be staying with Andrea who was in the room next to Popla *and* Bernard.

Gwendolyn felt like kissing the tall, handsome pirate but she just thanked him.

"You're all that they say you are Errlus. No wonder Olivia left Popla to find you."

"You know Olivia?" Errlus asked.

"Yes. She is the reason my husband avoided a carpool and talked our son into attending that choral meeting with him. She almost seduced my husband but he got away. She found you I take it.?"

"She is quite the seductress. She is also with child. Unfortunately, the man she took up with has been treating her rather coldly."

"Isn't that man you, Errlus?"

"Yes." He rolled his eyes and added. "She is not my wife. But she was a good diversion for a while. Diversions get costly sometimes timewise even if a person can change time. There are limits.

"Olivia never saw any." Gwendolyn said somewhat exasperatedly. "We had been friends, and then she came onto my husband. This was before she took up with Popla. I think she craved a family life but did not know how to get it. Her own family had been abducted shortly after she was born. She was raised by her babysitter's family who I believe did not like her much. They spoiled her so as to have more time to themselves. She ended up latching on to the people that gave her some attention. As she got older, men gave her the most attention."

"She is a beauty."

"I was surprised she liked Popla so much. He was always so quiet, almost timid. He was devastated when she left."

"He still wants her back, correct?" Errlus asked hopefully.

"He never stopped loving her."

"Perhaps you can help me get those two back together."

"You want to have me help your pregnant girlfriend get back with a suicidal child-like man?" Gwendolyn asked.

"It'll just take a few well placed words and supposedly random meetings if all goes well. Are you 'in'?"

"If you help me get my husband and son back, I'll need to make sure she's preoccupied. I'm definitely 'in'."

Errlus liked Gwendolyn. She was witty and fun. His plans were falling into place.

CHAPTER 23

BABIES

When Olivia heard that Gwendolyn was in the complex, she brought her a basket of her favorite muffins, a vase of diamond-petalled flowers, and a small note saying, "Sorry for all the problems I caused you. Please forgive me." She left the tray outside Gwendolyn's door, knocked and hurried away.

Gwendolyn sent a note to Olivia. In it she wrote, "If you're truly sorry, join me for lunch tomorrow at the luncheonette by the aquarium and bring more muffins. –Gwen",

At the luncheonette Gwendolyn sat with Popla who she talked into joining her for company.

When Olivia walked in, Popla's face flushed and his eyes watched her every move as she walked slowly to the table.

"Hello Gwendolyn." Olivia said and passed her a smal basket. "Hello Popla. I didn't know you would be here as well." She patted him on the shoulder. "It is so very good to see you. You can't believe how much I have been thinking of you these days."

"You, Olivia," Popla said, "have been my reason for living since the first day I saw you."

Gwendolyn feigned a nagging back pain and bid the couple to have a good day and enjoy their lunch as she returned to her cabin. She took the muffins and asked Olivia to get her the recipe.

The two talked and answered each other's sentences for two hours. Popla was enchanted and glad to be alive. Olivia was grateful for his attention and loved his look of adoration which she felt she could never deserve but was so thankful to see. They talked about baby names and of Andrea and Dominick, about Errlus's angry outbursts and strange kindnesses. Olivia expressed concern over Errlus' grief over Johannah and how she herself felt more like furniture than a person with him. Popla told her about the fiery moon where Errlus hoped to save Johannah. He didn't tell her about the role he was asked to play. He skipped that part. He knew neither Olivia, Gwendolyn nor his mother would allow him to attempt to rescue Johannah; but it was something he knew now that he had to try, just to get Olivia back.

CHAPTER 24

DIAMOND LEGGOS

G wendolyn had been permitted to have a link to the Time Cell Corporation's files. She was somewhat surprised that Errlus' servers could access her father's highly secured information. She managed to get to the folders that contained information from the year 2059. She typed in "L-E-G-G-O-S" into the search engine. A number of variations popped up. She compared the image of the diamond blocks with the image of the Leggos in the ancient files. She zoomed in on the individual blocks, plugged the image into a drafting program that drew the "Top", "Side", and "Front" views. Considering the design, she knew that just a small amount of pressure could cause the blocks to separate, so she modified the design so that the thin holes that connected each piece could snap and lock into place with the help of a small ledge at the end of each hole clicking past a rim she designed on each protruding circle on the top side of the Leggo block.

Once the drafting program finished, she took the printouts to the engineering team in charge of the project. Engineers considered the modifications to be saved then they went to Errlus.

The blocks were to be cut from manmade diamonds that were created in ovens placed back millions of years and guarded by what would become a secret society of time-travelling monks. The ovens were placed in huge manmade mountains that looked natural so as to be undetected. Some were placed in pyramids. The manmade diamonds would be used to create a wall to prevent the wall of lava from reaching Johannah. The wall would have to be set in the settlement before it was colonized. Popla would be taught how to trigger the wall to rise and cut through it's moonscape ceiling. It would need to rise quickly to prevent rocks from ever hitting Johannah. Just before Errlus got to her, a piece of molten rock knocked her out, then the lava enveloped her. Afterwards, Errlus was sedated by Jason who knew that without a sedative, Errlus would fight him off and die trying to save Johannah who was hit by the wall of lava just before his son was rescued. Just as he sedated Errlus, the two feather-clad images had sprung into action according to video tape secured from the time cell. The position of the rescuers and those rescued had to be exact so that the placement of the diamond walls would protect and not hinder rescue attempts.

For centuries monks autoclaved pieces of carbon in ovens camouflaged in mountains, pyramids, dungeons, ocean caves, and underground settlements. Members of Errlus' group periodically checked on the progress. If an elder monk ever needed food or tools, all he had to do was etch the request on a flattened wall of polished rock with a certain signature and date. The polished message board was constantly checked, and every hundred years a crew of "monks" went back to check on it. The items that were requested would arrive the next day. Only certain monks could carve into it. If an Earthquake or eruption caused the stone to be dislodged, it would be remounted or given additional space on one of the 100-year checks (which were actually done in only a series of weeks in Errlus's time). If during a systematic check, the autoclave had been abandoned, "monks would be sent back in 20 year segments to find the cause of the abandonment and neutralize the damage to the monastery and the ovens that were creating manmade diamonds.

Eventually there were enough uncarved diamond blocks that three 21-foot-high triangular sections were completed. A crew arrived before the year 1 of the settlement on IO, the fiery moon that circled Jupiter along with Ganymede. It brought with them the last diamond block shipment needed. Immediately another crew started setting up camp and another crew started drilling into the ground where Johannah would be standing thousands of years in the future.

The diamond pieces were in place in a matter of a few weeks from the time Gwendolyn first designed the modified blocks. This was done by a team of engineers conducting a series of trips to the far past and back again. The next step involved training the man who would rescue Johannah.

CHAPTER 25

INSIDE THE PYRAMID

Popla was in the timecell travelling to the past before colonization of the fiery moon had taken place. When the timecell door opened, he was greeted by a few robed monks who explained how to trigger the rise of the diamond walls. They gave him a graphite staff to plunge into the soft dirt. The ground shook and up came the walls. There were three. They came up over his head by fifteen feet. The seal they created was perfect. He plunged the staff into the mound of moon rock and the walls slid down, back into their lubed diamond slot masked by a moonscape.

Soon he was back in another timecell which took him to the same exact location at a time thousands of years after the lava wall had covered the spot where Johannah and Atticus had been. Excavations to the level at which Johannah and Atticus had stood revealed that the diamond wall was still in place. Popla plunged the staff into the designated area. It worked again.

After a days rest, Popla was back in another timecell that was to be sent to the moon's time of volcanic activity. This was the mission that was extremely critical. He was again dressed in the costume that Errlus had first seen him wearing. It appeared that there had been two images similarly dressed in the broad screen of the video that

Errlus had initially shown to Bernard, Andrea, Popla, and himself. Bernard and Andrea had seen only the narrow view of the rescue attempts. The wider view showed a shorter image standing in front of Johannah with a staff. The shorter, feathery creature looked like Popla.

The time cell stopped. The noise outside was thunderous. The door opened to a hot world of flying rocks. A woman stood just 4 feet from the ship's opening. Popla lunged toward her with the staff and stabbed the ground beside her feet as he grabbed her arm. The staff hit nothing. Johannah screamed. Popla said, "Please Mrs. Errlus, I've got to find just the right place." in such a calm, methodical voice that she realized Errlus must have sent him. He thrust the staff full force where she had been standing. The ground shook. A wall of lava was coming towards him but then the ground opened up to a row of thin diamond leggos. They glinted back the sparks of lava and rose to form a pyramid encapsulating, Johannah, himself and the time cell. He motioned for Johannah to enter the time cell, then pushed the buttons that would take them to the future time just after the excavation of the cooled lava and just before the practice-diamond wall activation test. They were in the cell for twenty minutes. At first it seemed rather warm. When the spinning of the time cell stopped it was 150 years from the time they had entered the cell. Johannah and Popla stepped out into the prism that contained them. It was beautiful. The sun created a rainbow effect that criss-crossed itself inside the giant diamond they were part of. Popla struck the ground in the designated area. Nothing. He tried again to no avail. He sat down.

"Here, let me try said Johannah." She struck the dirt with all her might in the area that she had been standing. She remembered it had a slight protrusion to it. She twisted the staff and the ground shook as the diamond walls slid back into the ground like fangs receding into a giant's gumline. How changed it all was Johannah noted. There were trees in the distance and streams of water.

"I wonder if Errlus got all the gold yet." She mused while looking to see that the encampments were more like homes now.

"Why didn't Errlus come himself you amazing masked man?" she asked.

"He died once trying." Said Popla. "Apparently, a person disappears if they return to the scene of their recent death."

"Makes sense." She said as she looked around. "Are there people waiting for us somewhere here?"

"That house over there with the smoke rising from the chimney… We're to go there. Tomorrow we take a ship to Ganymede. The next day we head to Earth. Then we go back in time to where Errlus will be waiting."

"My husband must trust you a lot to depend on you so much."

Popla for the first time realized how true this statement was. Errlus trusted him a great deal. He disliked Errlus for taking Olivia's attentions away from him, but he did respect him. And to have earned Errlus's respect, made him feel a strange sense of pride in his own abilities.

"Some of us would move mountains for the women we love. In that, Errlus and I are the same."

Johannah smiled, a calm, disarming smile and added, "A diamond mountain at that."

They talked like old friends as they walked to the small cottage.

CHAPTER 26

PRIMARY DIRECTIVE

The reception on Earth was a three day event. Popla was a hero. Olivia welcomed him with her five-day old newborn. While he was on Ganymede with Johannah, she had gone into labor. She was the first person Popla saw when the space ship door opened. She looked radiant. The crowd cheered, "Popla!" "Popla! "Popla!"

Popla resolved at that moment to make sure that if he ever had a son, he would not name him Popla. "Pavlov" or "Patrick" but not "Popla". Olivia had named her baby Naomi after her mother. She had discussed it with Popla before he left and he loved the name. He asked her to marry him that day as she put a wreath of flowers around his neck. She said, "Yes".

Johannah was welcomed with two bouquets of roses carried by her 12-year old son Atticus and a very tall woman dressed in feathers. Billy Joe was there promoting a movie of the rescue. Atticus was a welcome sight. The last time she had seen him a wall of lava was coming toward both of them. She thanked Billy Joe for her bravery. Billy Joe thanked her for her health and the inspiration Johannah had offered her.

When Johannah saw Errlus with his bouquet of flowers, the world seemed to go quiet. People were cheering and noisemakers were going off but all she heard was her husband saying, "Welcome home."

She smiled her calm peaceful way and said, "So, am I younger than you yet?" He laughed and said, "Yes, finally by at least a year." They kissed hello and then greeted the others.

Andrea's husband had been flown in. He was astounded by the engineering of the mid-ocean hideaway. Unfortunately, he had to greet Andrea in a prison cell. She had been constantly bombarding Errlus with insults and indignant requests to get Popla back from the mission. She was furious that he would put Popla in such danger. She could not be calmed. Doctors decided to sedate her till Popla returned. When Dominick was let in the cell he hugged her and told her that Popla had just returned and he was fine. She hugged Dominick and started to sob with relief.

Bernard wanted Gwendolyn to see the festivities but he wanted her safe. She was eight months into her pregnancy and he did not want her jostled. He arranged to have her sit in a wheelchair while they greeted Popla. When Bernard saw Popla he was surprised at how mature he seemed. They shook hands like old friends.

Eventually Gwendolyn would see her husband and son again. Errlus' crew had gone back to that day when her husband was to get into the car with her son. They arranged to have both of them stalled for a few minutes by a street musician's inquiry, then they made it appear that someone hijacked their car. A remote control device placed in the car made it follow the same path that Gwendolyn's husband and son would have taken. It appeared that they died in that firey crash as they had originally. Instead, they were rushed to a time cell location and eventually transported to Ganymede, the moon where Errlus was born. There, they would be given a home and taught the history and asked to wait for Gwendolyn.

Bernard knew he would lose Gwen soon after she delivered the baby but it was better than her being banished as her father would have done. Gwendolyn was to receive a place of honor in the Time Cell Corporation on Ganymede. She had helped save Johannah by designing diamond Leggos that held back a wall of lava. She and her husband and son would live there, on Ganymede, for the rest of their lives. Bernard could even write her via Time Cell Mail. It took messages back and forth in time along with supplies for developments.

The son she would deliver soon after the festivities would be named after Bernard's father Harry. The newborn had strawberry-blonde hair just like his mother. Gwendolyn had asked Bernard to raise the child for her as his own even if it turned out that the baby belonged to the man who had raped her. Bernard felt honored to be given the responsibility. Jonas, Gwendolyn's father volunteered babysitting time as did Dominick and Andrea, Popla and Olivia. They became like family.

Years later, when tumors started forming on the young boy's limbs, Bernard knew the boy was actually his. Odd to feel happy about such a thing but it meant that Harry was actually his son as well as Gwen's. He wrote her a note. She would get it someday. Harry was cured with the same treatment used on Bernard. Technology in that future time cured anything: suicide, volcanic eruptions, cancer, everything but a father's stubborn adherence to outdated convictions. Due to his convictions, Jonas lost his daughter to a past world but it was those same convictions that helped create that world and the one on which he lived. Harry became his life and Bernard became like a son to him. It seemed for Jonas, as Bernard had believed, that men of strong character and conviction are rarely left totally alone.

Errlus had his wife, Johannah, with him and now he was ready to go ahead to the next check point with his family. It would be the year 5097 Earth time. Errlus' next birthday would celebate 39 years of his life. His wife was now 1 year younger than him and his son would soon be a teenager. It was great to get things back to a pattern. In three more years, he would jump ahead to 6005, then three years later he would jump ahead to 6013. If he lived to be 159, he might see the seventh millenium. His son would probably see it. It was his hope that Atticus would keep the pattern; but if he didn't, the syndicate would be set up to continue the funding of the colonies. It was all written in the bible from Ganymede. It's good to have a direction, he thought to himself. He just hoped that he could follow the written word in a way that would benefit all people in Ganymede, IO, and on Earth in the Past, Present, and Future colonies. That was the primary directive. The years went by quickly.

CHAPTER 27

THE TIME PIRATE'S FIRST TRIP

For as long as anyone could remember, after the 17-year old son of their benefactor disappeared, the daughters of their world were sent to schools that were named after their benefactor's future daughter-in-law. This was because of a prank the 17-year old's best friend played on him centuries ago. While the two boys were checking out the lab where the Time Cell was stored, the younger boy slipped in through the partly opened door. Before exiting, he hit a bunch of numbers on the control board, laughed, then ran out just as his friend tripped in through the door to see what he was doing.

Both were stunned when the opening sealed shut. The boy who was left behind, told the elders how he watched the Time Cell become transparent, then disappear. He did not know when the Time Cell would reappear.

Due to a letter written to their benefactor, sent by the man who first used the Time Cell, it became known that once the boy who tripped into the Time Cell re-emerged into history, he would meet his future wife and both of them would lead their world into existence... and prosperous, honorable adventures. For this reason, centuries of young girls fell in love with the idea of being the reason that the benefactor's son chose to stay and take on the goals that were set for him to accomplish. Most girls were given the same first name since that was all that was known of the girl who enchanted the young man so much that he gave up his family and friends for her. Schools were set up to accommodate all who wished to have a chance to be the first heiress of their world. The schools were called, "Johannah Schools".

The letter written to their benefactor also instructed him to create their series of colonies on their Earthlike moon. The letter emphasized how the boy in the Time Cell, the benefactor's eldest son, would reappear in a future time, meet the love of his life, and stay in that future time because of her; and she would become his confidant, his resting place, his best friend. She was the link that would allow for the existence of the colonies because this boy would be trained to lead his future world back to Earth in a quest to re-populate the once uninhabitable planet with volunteers from the colonies on their world. These volunteers would also be trained to deal with a scorched planet and get it to yield crops again.

Earth had been the home of all the original colonists. At a future time, when the benefactor's son would be instructed by a visitor from his past, he would send ships to the time just before the Earth caught fire like a small sun. The ships would rescue the ancestors of the colonists and bring them to their new world where air, water, animal and plant life had been secured by the Time Pirate's men for centuries before his birth. The Johannah this 17 year old would meet had to be skilled; thus, the series of schools that were set up to teach the future spouse of a future leader demanded qualified applicants. Only the brightest, most well-rounded students were mandated to attend. All who attended had to have the highest grades in the colonies. Math, Science, Psychology, Physics, Statistics, Music and Art had to be mastered. Each attendee was also taught the value of being a good wife. They were taught how to cook using vegetables grown nearby. They were taught the history of two different worlds.

They were given courses in therapy so as to learn how to temper their own goals and how to soothe the temperaments of others. Then, once they mastered their classes, in the year before they graduated, the finest students were given a week in the lab in the hope that when the son of the man who brought them to this world appeared after stumbling and then traveling in an unsecured Time Cell, he would see "the Johannah of the week", fall in love, and continue with the plans set forth by his father over 1600 years before.

Most young women looked forward to their chance to become a woman loved by a mysterious, handsome man who would have the power to command scientists, engineers, bankers, and politicians. But a few women fell in love with the education more than the myth. Their waiting week for them was not a welcome way to spend their time. It was dreaded. One such woman was in the lab that day.

She remembered how her sister came home in tears at the end of her week. She had talked about him for years before. "He's so gorgeous?" "...so noble", "so wise..." "—he loved her so much!", "I heard he moved mountains for her." "She was his reason to be." This defiant woman's broken-hearted sister, Johannah Patricia Fyre, had been in love since she had heard his story like so many girls of that time were in love with the idea and the chance to be married to someone so perfect. She, however, thought that the entire idea was annoyingly manipulative and limiting. For centuries, girls thought of him hoping their week in the lab would reap them a mythical husband. They would don their white lab coats and take their turn. She refused to go by her first name (which like the others was "Johannah"). Her name was Fiorin Fyre. She would not answer her mother till she called her Fiorin even when only her and her mother were in the room. She wanted to be a physicist. "Forget marriage!" she told her family. "Science is more important." She was anxious for her week to be over. She did not want to be just a wife to some future hero. She wanted to be known for her discoveries not just as a loved spouse.

She had dreaded the idea of meeting him: she had figured he would be spoiled and snobbish. Soon, this last day would be over, this week of mandatory waiting, and her time of being subjected to an already chosen fate, would be done. She could focus on her Physics degree without interruption. Her sister's last opportunity in the lab was met with devastation but "Fiorin Fyre", felt elated. She looked anxiously at the digital clock.

Nearly 100 people in white lab-coats were with her in the huge three-story lab. Photographers were busy trying to set-up their cameras in key locations. A young man came over to her and stated the obvious: "Your time here is almost done." To his surprise, she told him how she could not wait. "My sister was devastated when her time ended. I'll be so relieved." She looked at the door anxiously. "Why pink?" the young man asked, indicating the color of her lab coat. Fiorin stated, "I was hoping to get my mother to let me stay home by making sure all my lab coats got bleached with a red scarf. She just made me wear one. I'll be glad to just go back to studying. This waiting for a mythical husband is wasting my time."

Just then the light fluttered, and a hissing sound from the platform area started as a pinkish-golden ball appeared spinning and spraying a shower of steam and mist over the closest crowd. Everyone cheered and flashes from cameras went off like fireworks. The young man looked at "Johannah" Fiorin, and said, "I was about to ask you out...." As he looked at the emerging glowing orb, "but it looks like you're engaged." He bowed away from her.

She was horrified and wanted to escape. She walked to the nearby restroom, tried the windows, started for the door, but guards were blocking her way. Photographers started taking her picture. The golden orb stopped spinning, a door hissed open in the object, and out stepped a young boy.

He looked puzzled at all the people taking pictures and cheering. He saw a pretty girl in pink staring at him and walked toward her. She was the only one not cheering or clapping. He reached her and asked "What's all the fuss?" She looked at his handsome boyish face and suddenly realized, "his family is gone. He has no one. His mother and father, sister, brothers have been dead for centuries but to him they are still alive. He was only gone 15 minutes...."

"You don't know... do you?!" she asked incredulously.

She thought of how he would never see his family again. This stung her. How could she tell him? Her heart became overwhelmed with compassion and loss as if his family's passing brought her grief also. She took his hand and said, "Well..." She looked into his amazing eyes and was taken-back by the way he looked at her. "I have so much to tell you."

The warmth of her hand was so reassuring. She was so calm and so concerned for some reason as if some great sadness had come over her; but her smile made everything everywhere seem to have a purpose. He asked her her name. She—for the first time in her 18 years of life—said her first name proudly. "Johannah" she said. If he was her fate, predicted by folk songs, bibles, children stories, history books, she would accept whatever that fate would bring. He needed someone to show him the value of himself and the value of the work laid out for him by his father. He would be the leader that would bring them back to Earth some day. He would need a reason to believe in all he had to do. Somehow she knew she was now that reason and the innocence and joy she saw in his face when he arrived after his short journey to a new time, fascinated her. She was falling in love; and so was he. Gingerly, she led him to the door and opened it to a city he had never seen that had waited for him since the day he should have turned eighteen.

ABOUT THE AUTHOR

The author and her fiancé on vacation in 2009

Catherine Weiss-Celley – for 12 years – had worked on temporary assignments as a draftsman and technical writer. The work included centerline light configurations for airfields, pipe layout for water companies, signage for government buildings, HVAC Control drawings as well as architectural and civil drawings. She is also a former assistant director of a local poets' group, a caricature artist, illustrator and painter. She resides in Southeastern Pennsylvania with her fiancée, Jim Goslin, near the homes of her children, and relatives (a family of roofers, electricians, secretaries, waitresses, social workers, and office personnel). There she enjoys taking part in the many family-oriented activities available: barbecuing, some rare times: boating, going to local exhibits or street fairs, reunions with cousins, dinners or movies with family and friends. Recently, she had found time to complete "ERRLUS" which initially was to be a series of small books.

ERRLUS.., has been in the works since the mid-80's. It was to be the middle section of a series of three books: (1) MAN FROM THE PAST; (2) ERRLUS: The Time Pirate; and (3) JOHANNAH-The Time Pirate's Wife: Back to the Fiery Moon. The beginning of this compilation was about to be shelved for dust collection until a good friend of the author's, *Eve Kirsten Blakely,* published a poem titled: *"Outside Tea Party"* © in 1990. It was based on two childhood friends of Eve's who ended their lives too abruptly. They both came from what the author had thought was a wealthy neighborhood, but the 13-year old boy who played at Eve's tea-parties did not want to shoot wrens with his father after receiving a rifle for Christmas. The entire poem is printed below. Eve was hesitant to have only an excerpt of the poem be printed. May the souls of those mentioned here find peace and guidance from the maker of all things. This poem is included to honor their memory and the lives of those who may have felt at some time in their lives, as they had felt.

OUTDOOR TEA PARTY ©
(for Larry Ramaika and Linda Opfer)

Even in death my father
kept hold of me,
never let go;
the night my friend died,
swallowed the bullet that spread
the insides of his young head
all over his bed,
so red,
like the morning of a girl's
first period,
he told me how he shot his toe
long ago.

My best friend
so quickly dead at thirteen,
one shot
in whose wake the neighborhood
undulates;
my mother helping the others who
congregate like Quaker women,
scrapes his brains
into a crimson bucket;

All this
just to hear a childhood story,
just to lie
in my father's arms,
see the tiny scar on his toe.
Even the moon sways
lays a shroud
on the furious flash of sirens

flailing their beet-red arms
against our drapes
like frightened bird wings,
rhythmic as this rocking.

At nine years old,
the little boy next door's suicide
seems almost a lie
another myth conspired by adults
like Santa, God.
No St. Nick left that rifle,
a gift from his father
who needed a son to hunt with,
shoot wrens,
not play with younger girls
like a sissy;
but it was always we three:
Larry, Linda, and me
playing tea party.

He hung the pungency of maleness
above our coddled, girlish lives,
a raven amidst doves
he taught important things
like how to climb trees,
read Jabberwocky,
shoot BBs."

Never again did I
feel such love
from my father
as that night,

as he beat at the bloodscreaming
lights
like at a garret bat
loose in the house.

But life rushed to fold
back in on itself
like tight petals;
with the help of the moon
it could pretend
there was still a flower within.
And my father could comfortably
refuse to discard that red bucket,
make my mother still use it
to scrub floors.

Is it any wonder
I hoarded pills like acorns
all those years,
occasionally swallowing
a bottle or two;
but it always rolled off him
like dew on a waxy leaf;
like this new hole
did on Linda,
who went to school the very next day,
Shirley Temple curls still in place,
even played at recess.

Years later,
Linda shot herself,
at twenty-one,
with a handgun.

"Flanked by suicides
I'm still alive,
even though I was the one
they all thought would go;
and I still have the photograph
my father shot
of Larry, Linda, and me
summered and smiling;
an outdoor tea party."

Eve Kirsten Blakely
—1990 © copyright – Eve Kirsten Blakeley

Ms. Weiss- Celley after hearing the poem and since having read about Japan's high suicide rates at that time and of other young people in the United States who gave up totally, decided to continue to write about a time when illness and money were no longer a problem but one-third of the world's children had signed up for the NR3, a room where a person could go inside, push a button and disappear in a flash of smoldering circuits. Errlus, the villain/hero/ time-pirate, becomes the catalyst of change for some of those NR3 candidates. He ends up *using* them in ways they could never have imagined.

Errlus is pronounced like errorless without the middle syllable. ['er-lus – (i.e.: "er" as in "error" and "lus" as in "lust"; a name that is intended to represent a person who is errorless)]

This book offers insight into the motivations of a powerful, conscientious people driven by circumstances that seem orchestrated by an elaborate program spanning thousands of years. The NR3, the third death chamber of its kind, fuels this "orchestration" in ways only Errlus and people with key positions in his syndicate can comprehend. Read the book to find out the motivation of a desperate, powerful man who seems to live forever.

AUTHOR'S NOTE

When I was a teenager, a young boy who I would sometimes talk to while waiting for a clear tennis court at the playground, came to my house looking upset. He was anxious about something. I was surprised he knew where I lived. All I knew about him was he was an excellent tennis player. Some day I hoped he would teach me more about tennis when he had the time. He was known for winning tournaments even though he was young. One person told me he was 13; someone else told me he was 9.

I always brought my sketch book to the tennis courts and sometimes drew the people there in small sketches. The sketching was part homework, part wanting to fill time, part wanting to feel special because I could draw somewhat well.

This boy had a bunch of questions for me. Most important to him seemed to be the question of "Why" I brought my sketchbook with me. First I told him that my art teacher told the class to sketch something everyday. He said, "But you bring it even in the summer." I said, "Well, I have to go back in the Fall to the same teacher." He said that he thought that the main reason I brought the book was to "show off." I tried to point out other reasons but he seemed so insistent. I would have invited him in but I didn't want him to see my messy house. My mother was at work, my three brothers and sister were home and they were making a commotion in the background. I figured he might just be right: perhaps I was showing off so I said, "Yes, I guess I was showing off a little."

He said, "Fine. I knew it." And he left.

A few weeks later I found out that that boy went to a field a block and a half from my house and shot himself. I am not sure if it was the same day he came to my house. I often wonder if I had said something else, been more friendly (even though the house was a mess), offered him a glass of water, or said, "No, I just like to draw." And sounded sincere would he have gotten through whatever was bothering him that day.

Some people said his mother and father were getting a divorce. Divorce then was less accepted than it is now. I don't know if that was the trigger.

This book explores some of the reasons for suicide: inadequacy, loss, cold attitudes, joblessness, lack of feeling proud— these things cause suicidal natures. Now-a-days with joblessness being so rampant, more people may succumb to this last choice in a life. I figure suicide is like slapping God in the face with all the gifts he gave us: the sky, air, coolness, warmth, friendship, love, lust, taste—so many gifts. It's like saying, "the gifts are not enough!" It's like taking God's works of art, throwing them down on the ground, and jumping on them or rolling over them with a steam roller. Of course those that come to that point are not thinking correctly. I pray that the souls of these people are allowed better options in the next realm of existence. No one can truly know what type of realm that will be: reincarnation, ghost-work, heaven.

This boy woke me up to the emptiness some people feel. There were times when I also felt like there was "nothing" meaningful or worthwhile but these were brief moments erased by a breeze, an errand, a memory. I wasn't sure if other people felt this sense of worthlessness or vacuum of meaning like I sometimes did back then. At least, I wasn't sure until this boy ended his young life.

Sometimes art can fill a void; or a teacher or friend can be the link to the next worthwhile moment in a life. It is a shame to waste a life. I wish I could have helped this young tennis player back then and now all I can do for him is pray that his soul finds some solace and honor in the accomplishments he did achieve at a young age.

He has been in my thoughts often throughout my life. He was the first inspiration for me to write this book. I keep wondering what I could have said or done to help. Maybe his spirit will find some joy in knowing he is remembered.